PRAISE
FOR
MISERY LOVES COMPANY

"In Misery Loves Company, B. Lawson Thornton tells a compelling, emotionally charged story that is sure to keep you glued to each page and starving for more."

- Nikki Turner: The Princess of Hiphop Fiction, Essence Bestselling author of "A Hustler's Wife" and "A Project Chick"

"You don't know drama until you've read this novel. Kerri Mitchell experiences it all as she juggles fake friends and men that ain't worth a damn. B. Lawson Thornton brings the realness."

- Marlon Green, author of "Butter" and "Making Love in the Rain"

"Misery Loves Company is a true to life, inspirational tale that will have the reader wondering what Kerri is up to next! B. Lawson Thornton gives a gutwrenching account of a young Black woman struggling to survive inner city life by any means necessary against almost insurmountable odds. Kerri's story is one that many women who have been trapped in a cycle of unhealthy and abusive relationships can relate to and use as a source of strength in regaining their self-respect. This is an excellent first novel and I look forward to much more in the future from this rising star in the literary field."

- Thomas Long, author of "Reflections of My Soul" and "For My Sisters: 7 Relationship Tips"

THIS BOOK IS PUBLISHED BY:
East River Press, L.L.C.
P.O. Box 4615
Largo, MD 20775

Second Printing July 2003

ISBN 0-9740183-0-9

1. African-American Fiction. 2. Battered Women - Fiction.
3. Domestic Violence - Fiction. 4. Depression - Fiction.
5. Alcoholism - Fiction. 6. Teenage Pregnancy - Fiction.

Printed in the United States of America

PUBLISHER'S NOTE:
This is a work of fiction. Names, characters, places and
incidents either are the products of the author's imagination
or are used fictitiously, and any resemblance to actual
persons, living or dead, events, or locales is entirely
coincidental.

Price:
$15.00 USA
$20.00 Canada

ACKNOWLEDGMENTS

Heavenly Father, thank you for granting me the serenity to accept the things I cannot change, the courage to change the things I can, and the wisdom to know the difference.

All that I am, I owe to my mother, Dorinda Thornton and my grandmother, Bernice E. Thornton. Without your love and guidance over the years, I don't know what would have become of me.

To my Lawson family, especially Aunt Darlene, thank you for supporting my book from day one. When everyone else laughed, you all listened. Your constant encouragement gave me the extra push I needed.

William T. Lawson, my loving father, the bond we share is unbreakable.

Amerah and Percillah, my precious gifts, you bring mommy so much joy. My love for you is everlasting.

Danielle a.k.a. Muffin, though we didn't get to know each other until adulthood, I treasure the relationship we've developed. You are truly more than a cousin, you're a cherished friend.

Dearest friends Keisha Cofield, Lakesha Lee, Muminah Al Jabar a.k.a. Turwanna, and Tina Nickleberry, oh how I love each of you. Four unique women...four distinct friendships, all special for different reasons. You each share one common quality, your unconditional love for me.

Keisha, a talented artist and gifted inventor, I have one question...where are my candles?

Lakesha, remember when we sat at my dining room table and ate fried smoked sausages...can we do that again real soon?

Muminah, true friends don't need to speak everyday...we sometimes go for months without talking, but whenever I need you, you are always there for me.

Tina, I'm so glad to have met you...who would have thought we'd become as close as we are, nine years is a long time...but who's counting?

A very special thank you goes to my attorney, Isaac N. Edoga...your legal advice was most valuable; to Roy Cox for putting up with my daily phone calls and no-doubt annoying emails...through it all you remained professional and patient...you're definitely the best photographer I know; to Carolyn Edwards of Pretty Faces...thanks for hooking me up with your flawless make-up services.

Darren Coleman, I'm so glad you answered Lakesha's email! From the very moment we met, you showed me nothing but love. The time you spent talking, encouraging, and guiding me is greatly appreciated. You not only promote your book, you promote mine as well...you're a first class author and an even better friend.

Marlon Green, thanks to my other friend, Keisha, I had the pleasure of making your acquaintance. In the brief time that I've known you, you've been nothing short of supportive, your vast knowledge of writing and the publishing process has enlightened me and I'm honored to call you my friend.

To Marlon Cash, thank you for being my knight in shining armor...you came through when I needed you...for that, I am forever grateful.

Finally, I would like to thank everyone who read my manuscript and encouraged me to publish my first novel. Thanks to all of you, I have graduated from writer to published author.

Sincerely,

B. Lawson Thornton

MISERY LOVES COMPANY:

The Diary of Kerri Mitchell

A Novel By
B. Lawson Thornton

An East River Press Book

B. Lawson Thornton

CHAPTER ONE

It was the first Sunday of the new year. I hadn't been to church in months and was eager to attend Sunday morning service. There is always something special about the first sermon of the year. After all, it is generally said that the first couple of days of the new year are a sample of the rest of the year to come. I had been through so much hell the previous year that I just knew this year would bring better experiences. Later that day, I would learn that my troubles were about to start all over again.

After attending one of the best Sunday services ever, I decided to pay my grandmother a visit. We usually talked several times a week, but I had been so busy that I hadn't called her in a few days and knew she would be happy to see me.

Grandma's house was the absolute place to be on any given Sunday. Everyone in the family would drop in for the latest gossip and to savor grandma's down home cooking. I spotted three relatives' cars as I searched for a place to park my ride.

Being at grandma's house was like being on the set of a first-rate sitcom. Uncle Squirt, kicked out of his house when he caught his wife in bed with another man, was at constant disagreement with cousin Netta, who had moved into grandma's house after being fired from her fifth job in one year. Then there was cousin Joe who'd just been released from prison, and aunt Pam with her four children. All the characters were there. If I didn't know any better, I would've thought grandma's house was the city shelter.

I rang the bell and cousin Netta answered, "Well if it ain't the devil herself," she said as she closed the door behind me.

"Whatever, Netta. You just mad because I have a job," I said.

"I know, Kerri. She just mad because you have a job," said uncle Squirt.

"You need to stop worrying about me and start worrying about your whore, oops, I mean, your wife," Netta said to Squirt.

"Alright now! That's enough. I'm not gonna have all that loud talking in my house!" Grandma yelled.

Before I could even sit down, the telephone rang. Without so much as a hello, Randall, my whacked-out, cracked-out, soon to be exed-out husband, was on the phone screaming at the top of his lungs and yelling every obscenity known to man. He was mad as hell. In fact, he was furious. I hadn't heard him speak to me in that tone and manner in years, ever since he stopped beating me. Although I could hardly decipher what terrible act I was accused of committing, I did manage to hear the word prostitute.

After listening to him curse and rave for more than ten minutes, I slammed the phone down. Just then, it hit me. That damn Joanne! At some point that morning, my roommate Joanne had gotten a hold of Randall and spilled the beans. *That sneaky bitch. How dare she?* I thought to myself. I had always had my suspicions of her, but telling Randall my most intimate secrets was the last straw.

Before I went to church that morning I told Joanne that the roommate situation was not working out and that I wanted her to leave. She admitted that she had been sensing some tension and felt it was time for her to get her own place as well. I agreed and left for church. Driving in my car, I thought to myself *You see, that wasn't so bad after all.*

I had been debating whether to kick Joanne out, but I didn't want to ruin our friendship so I never said a word. I was hoping that my feelings would change or, better yet, she'd leave on her own. That never happened. Instead, I discovered that my suspicions of her were true - that she really wasn't the true friend I wanted her to be, that she really was jealous of what little success I had achieved, and that she truly did want me to be as miserable as she was. For the entire eight years that I knew Joanne, I suspected all these things about her, but, for whatever reason, I chose to ignore what I knew to be the truth.

Sometimes in life we allow ourselves to believe in people and things that we know are not true. We put our faith and trust in people only to be disappointed time and time again. You would think that sooner or later, we'd get tired of being let down and disappointed and be inspired to become uplifted and encouraged. But too many times, we don't. We create a pattern of mistakes and bad choices and ultimately suffer the consequences of our own misjudgments.

After realizing that Joanne had told Randall all the saucy details of my most sordid secrets, I was enraged. I was so embalmed with anger that I had an irresistible desire to stick my foot up Joanne's ass. "She's dead! Her ass is mine!" I said with fury. "I took that back-stabbing bitch in when no one else would, not even her own damn family!" I screamed out loud while speeding down the Baltimore/Washington Parkway. "I've got to get home. Why are these cars moving so slow?" I was flying down the Baltimore/Washington Parkway, weaving in and out of lanes like an Indy race car driver. I just couldn't believe it. How could the one person I trusted betray me this way? It just wasn't fair. Life wasn't fair. It seemed as if every time I got on the right track, some inexplicable bullshit would come along and throw me back on the other side. *When is the drama gonna stop?* I wondered.

Before pulling into the parking lot, I scanned every space for Joanne's car. I didn't see it so I went in the house. Boy was she lucky. I had planned to flatten the tires and bust the windows of any and every car that even looked like hers.

Once in the house, I went into the pantry to get the bolt lock I kept on standby. During the time that Randall and I were together, I had changed my locks so many times that it was second nature for me to keep a spare lock handy. So, I got my toolbox from under the kitchen sink, changed the locks on my front door and called one of my closest friends, Jamillah.

First, I tried calling her at home, then I called her cell phone. She answered, "What's up Kerri?"

"Hey, Jamillah, are you busy right now?" I couldn't wait to tell her what had just happened.

"I was on my way to my mother's house," She said.

"No, I need you to come over here right now. I'm gonna kill this bitch!"

"Kerri, what's wrong? Who are you going to kill?"

"That damn Joanne! She has really done it this time!" That was all I needed to say. Jamillah was there in less than 10 minutes. That's why I called her. She had always been there when I needed her, no matter what the situation was.

Jamillah was the one person I knew would be down with kicking Joanne's ass. She never liked her anyway.

I also called two of my cousins, Monica and Melanie. Out of all my female cousins, we were the closest and I knew they had my back.

Jamillah arrived first. She had the prettiest, whitest teeth you'd ever want to see. Her creamy dark chocolate skin and hourglass figure could turn the gayest motherfucker straight. And her down-to-earth persona would make you want to be her friend for life. But don't let the good looks and mild manner fool you. Though she looked sweet and innocent, that girl could beat the pants off Mike Tyson.

Jamillah had on a tan linen suit. She was dressed to the nines. I took one look at her and said, "Oh no, honey, take that suit off! You have to put on some rumbling gear."

"For who? Joanne? Chile please. Her sucka ass couldn't fight her way out of a paper bag." We both laughed at the thought. Then Jamillah's attitude switched from playful to concerned. "So what happened? I mean what did Joanne do to make you so mad?"

"That stinkin' bitch went and told Randall that I was a prostitute!"

"She did what?"

"Did I stutter?"

"Girl, stop it. I know Joanne ain't go there!"

"Yes, she did, honey!"

"Why would she tell him that?"

"Beats me. I guess she was mad because I told her she had to leave."

"Wait a minute…so you finally gave her the boot?" Jamillah walked into the kitchen and grabbed a bag of potato chips from the countertop. "When did all of this happen?"

"This morning."

"Girl, stop it! So you finally told her to get her shit and go, huh?"

"Yes, I mean I just couldn't take it no more. She was getting on my last fucking nerve!"

We sat in the living room on the couch exchanging words. "So how did you find out that Joanne talked to Randall?" Jamillah's hands were glued to the bag of chips, and her ears were suctioned to my lips, savoring my every remark. It was like she was listening to the dialogue of one of those melodramatic daytime soap operas.

"He called me at my grandmother's house. Girl I was pissed."

"So what else did she tell him?" Jamillah asked while stuffing a handful of chips in her mouth.

"She told him a whole bunch of shit. She even told him about Sherman."

"Oh no, she didn't!"

"Oh yes, she did!"

"I just can't believe it. Joanne should know better." Jamillah was so busy getting her fill of gossip, and I was so busy dishing the dirt that I didn't even realize she had knocked over her cup and spilled red juice all over my beige carpet.

"Yeah, girl. I can't believe it either. That bitch just told all my damn business. She put me out there like a mo'fo. She told Randall that I stole money from him and even went so far as to tell him where I hid it!"

"Girl, you have got to be kidding me. I told you to watch that bitch. I knew she was the type to pull a dope fiend move but goddamn! She really outdid herself this time."

"That's just what I heard before I hung up the phone on him. God knows what else she told him!"

I was outraged. All I wanted was for Joanne to come walking through that door. I was going to kick her ass until I couldn't kick it no more. I was looking out the window trying to spot her like some deranged lunatic waiting for the precise moment to strike. I kept waiting, but Joanne never came. I then went to her bedroom and started to gather her clothes from the closet.

"What the hell are you doing?" Jamillah was shocked to see me tearing through Joanne's closet.

"I'm getting her shit out of here!" I said spitefully.

"Kerri, think about what you're doing. You don't want to go to jail. Just let her come and get her shit and we'll get somebody from around the way to kick her ass."

Jamillah tried her best to talk some sense into me, but I wouldn't listen.

"Kerri, you know Joanne is scared to death. She's not coming back here. Just put her stuff in a nice little pile outside your door."

"Whatever. I'm going to put her stuff in a pile alright, right outside the trash! I know she's not foolish enough to come back here after doing some cruddy shit like that, so I have to fuck her up mentally. Therefore, all this shit has to go! Now stop with the logical BS and help me throw this shit in the dumpster!"

One by one and piece by piece, we emptied her closet. Everything she ever owned was in her there and it all went in the neighborhood dumpster.

After throwing her clothes out, I still wasn't satisfied. I realized that she could climb in there and get her stuff out, so I went back in the house and grabbed two jugs of bleach.

"Here, Jamillah, use this too!"

"What the hell is that?"

"Bleach, what does it look like?"

"Girl you crazy! But I don't blame you, she deserves it for what she did to you."

We proceeded to pour bleach over every thing in the dumpster. We went back in the apartment and started to remove the other miscellaneous objects from her room. Then someone knocked at the door. I just knew it was Joanne so I opened the door ready to kick some ass. It was Monica and Melanie. They came in and I started telling them what had happened and why I had called them over.

That was the beauty of it all. They all came over before they even knew what the problem was. All I had to say was that I needed them and there they were, ready for whatever forces that might be.

I had been dating Joanne's cousin Sherman. I called his mother's house to see if they knew where Joanne was and he answered the phone. "What's up, Sherman? Have you seen Joanne?"

"No, I haven't seen her."

"Okay, Sherman. Let me speak to your mother." I was determined to find Joanne and make her pay for what she had done.

Sherman passed the phone to his mother. "Hey Kerri, what's up?"

"Ain't shit. You seen Joanne?"

"No, I haven't seen her today. Do you want me to tell her to call you if she comes past?"

"No, but you can tell her that I'm gonna stick my foot up her ass when I catch her."

"What?" Sherman's mother was confused.

"You heard me. I'mma kick her ass," I said calmly.

"What is going on, Kerri?"

"Don't worry about it, it doesn't concern you. Just make sure you tell that bitch to watch her back." Click. I hung up the phone.

About thirty minutes later, Sherman called me back. He said he knew what had happened and that Joanne had just left his mother's house and was afraid to come home.

When I told Sherman what I did to Joanne's clothes he didn't believe me. "You did what?"

"You heard me. I threw all her shit in the trash."

"Everything?" Sherman asked in disbelief.

"I sure did. Why, you got a problem with that?"

"Nah, that's between you and Joanne. I ain't got nothing to do with it."

Sherman asked if he could come and get the rest of Joanne's things. I told him that whatever he could salvage he could have, but that practically everything she had left in my apartment had already been destroyed. Then Sherman's mother, Joanne's aunt, got on the phone. "Kerri, what is going on between you and Joanne?"

"I don't know. Why don't you tell me?" I said sarcastically.

"This is ridiculous. Y'all have been friends for a long time. The two of you need to sit down and talk this out."

"Fuck talking. We have nothing to talk about. Joanne has done me dirty for the last time. She was wrong and she knows it. And when I finish kicking her ass everyone else will know it too."

"Why did you throw her things in the trash?"

"Because that's exactly what she is, trash!"

" Kerri, doncha think this is just a bit juvenile?"

"I don't think it's juvenile at all. Running around tellin' people's husbands all sorts of lies about them is juvenile if you ask me."

"Well, I see that you are still upset. And I can't seem to talk any sense into you. Can the girl at least come and get what's left of her things?"

"Sure. She can come and get whatever she wants."

"Is there anything left for her to get?"

"Sure there is. It's all piled up by the dumpster."

It was a sight to behold. It looked as if the Sheriff had just evicted someone, but there was no Sheriff in sight. Just one fed up sistah on a serious mission to hurt someone who had hurt her one time too many.

CHAPTER TWO

It was an ending that many predicted. From the very first moment that I became friends with Joanne, practically everyone I knew told me to watch out for her because she could not be trusted. But as usual, I didn't listen. I never listened. I always had all the answers, damn what anyone else had to say. I wasn't interested in anyone else's opinion, just my own.

Come to think of it, half the heartache and misery I have endured over the years could have been prevented just by listening to some of the advice I was given. For instance, my grandmother always gave me good advice. Usually it went in one ear and out the other. Grandma or "Ma" as I call her, is the most generous, considerate person I know. Ours is a special relationship. I have always been her favorite. Even though she'd never admit to showing any favoritism, it's common knowledge. She practically raised me. Don't get me wrong, my mother raised me, but she could not have done it without my grandmother's help.

At the tender age of 16 my mother was into everything. Boys, cars, drugs and partying. One guy in particular caught her eye. His name was Kip. They never really had a relationship, just an occasional fling here and there. Kip was a ladies man. D.C.'s answer to Billy D. Williams. All the girls wanted a piece of him and they all got it, including my mother. But what set my mother apart from the other girls was that she got a piece of him literally - she became pregnant with me while in high school. Nine months later I was born. Fortunately, my mother did finish high school, but Kip did not share in this fortune. He went on to commit murder and was sentenced to life in prison.

Growing up without a father was hard. It became especially hard when my family discovered that my mother was sick. She suffered from clinical depression.

Depression, in its purest form, can be devastating. It is an illness that most people don't and essentially can't understand unless they have experienced it for themselves. I sure as hell didn't understand it. Neither did my mother. In the beginning of her illness, I didn't know what was going on. I just knew that something wasn't right, that whenever she'd have one of her spells I'd have to stay with a relative, usually my grandmother, until she got better.

I was about 7-years-old when my mother initially started having nervous breakdowns. It wasn't until I was a teenager that I started to really understand what my mother was going through.

Depression can stem from many things. In my

mother's case, I believe it was a mixture of previous drug use and her own chemical imbalance.

I remember one of my mother's episodes just as if it happened yesterday. I had come home from school and noticed that she hadn't been to work. She was laying in the bed in total darkness.

Whenever my mother felt depressed she would close up shop. I mean she would just lay around in the bed with the lights out, curtains drawn, no T.V., no radio, no nothing. Most times she wouldn't even bother to brush her teeth or wash her ass. She would completely shut down. I walked into her bedroom to see if she was okay. She wasn't. She was crying hysterically. She told me that she couldn't bear feeling that way anymore and that she was going to kill herself. I asked her what was wrong and she didn't answer me. After trying for about thirty minutes to find out what was bothering her, I just gave up. I put my arms around her and started to cry. We both lay there on her bed, wrapped in each other's arms and cried.

That was the first time I had actually seen my mother in her sickness. Here I was 12-years-old, and already I was given more responsibility than any child should ever have to bear.

At that time in my life things at home started to go haywire. My mother was constantly in and out of psychiatric treatment centers and I had begun to notice boys. I was in the seventh grade and had never seen that many boys in one place before. The junior high I attended was an open spaced school - meaning there were no classrooms, just one spacious room with dividers separating each class. You could see and hear the people in the next class. Since I had a short attention span and often got into trouble, that proved to be iniquitous.

One day my class attended an assembly. By the time we arrived at the auditorium it was nearly full to capacity. I looked around for some of my friends. While trying to locate them, I saw someone that looked familiar. I couldn't tell if it was him or not, so I walked back to where he was sitting.

The closer I got, the more I realized that it was him. I hadn't seen Devin since elementary school where he left two years before I did. We talked for a brief moment then I went to sit with my class.

After seeing Devin, I couldn't concentrate on the assembly. All I could think of was how happy I was to see him and how, some way or another, I was going to be his girlfriend.

I had always had a crush on Devin. He was two years older than me and was a good friend of my cousin Tony. Back in elementary, he and Tony would walk me to school.

I always wanted to be Devin's girlfriend, even in elementary school. He told me that I was too young for him and besides, he thought of me as a little sister, since he and my cousin Tony were so close. But that was then. I now had breast, big ones at that, and I had every intention to use them to catch whoever struck my fancy.

After the assembly Devin met me in the hall. We talked for a while and then exchanged phone numbers. I was ravished. Not only had I seen him, I now had his phone number. I could call him and tell him everything I had

always wanted to say; how I had liked him since grade
school, how cute I thought he was, and how I wanted him to
marry me. I was elated.

Devin and I got closer over the summer. He would
come to visit me at my house and vice versa. The first time
he visited me, we sat on the porch and talked. I couldn't
believe I had actually started a relationship with him. I
thought he would never give me a chance because I was
younger and because of his relationship with my cousin. I
was wrong. He was no longer concerned with my cousin or
my age, he was on a mission. The same mission that most
teenage boys are on. He wanted to fuck me. But there was
one problem. I was still a virgin and had no plans to become
sexually active.

Devin and I continued to see each other almost daily
that summer. Each day he would try something new in an
effort to get me to give in to his sexual advances. At first, I
wouldn't even kiss him. After a while I did. That satisfied
him somewhat, but he still wanted more. I started to feel
that he was only around to see if he could break me so I
stopped seeing him. I met a couple of other boys who were
interested in me and not sex and I talked to them instead.
Then school was back in session. I was now in the eighth
grade and Devin had started his first year of high school.

I started to see Devin again. Since he was attending
another school that made it easier for me. One day Devin
hooked school. It didn't seem like such a big deal so I
agreed to join him. I went to his house, which was about a
10 minute walk from my school. He hadn't changed one bit.
Before I could get one foot in the door he was all over me.
We stood near the foyer and kissed for what seemed like
hours. Then he went into his bedroom. Not fully realizing

what I was about to get myself into, I followed him much like a lioness trailing her perilous pride. The next thing I knew, we were buck naked, locking lips on his twin sized bed while the Whispers' hit single "In The Mood" blared from the cassette tape player.

Now you tell me, what in the hell were a 13-year-old girl and a 15-year-old boy doing listening to The Whispers and, more importantly, hooking school and having sex like two bona fide adults?

So it finally happened. After a year of persistent pressure I gave in. I gave in to sex and what would eventually turn into a 3-year drama of love him and leave him.

After my first sexual experience I wanted more and more. I would see Devin several times a week and each time we'd have sex. He was the only person I slept with, but I surely wasn't his only. He was sleeping with everybody, but I believed him when he said he wasn't.

My mother started to suspect that I was no longer a virgin. She never came out and asked me if I was sexually active and I never told her. She found out when I became pregnant with Devin's child. I was 14-years-old.

I knew I was pregnant, but I was afraid to tell anyone. Devin handled the news pretty well, but his mother was a different case.

Devin was his mother's only child, her sweet little boy. She thought I had planned to get pregnant just to steal his innocence. She didn't realize that her son was far from innocent. He was fucking every girl in town.

When my mother found out I was pregnant she was
outraged. She couldn't believe it. How did her little girl
stumble down the same road in which she had? She insisted
that I was too young to have a baby and made an
appointment for me to have an abortion.

Her first attempt at forcing me to have an abortion
failed. Our initial trip to the clinic ended abruptly. After
hearing what the doctor would have to do to my body in
order to terminate the pregnancy I refused to get undressed.
My mother, along with the nurse and doctor, tried to
persuade me to go through with the procedure but I wouldn't
budge. "There is no way I'm going through with that!" I
told them. So we went home and I remained pregnant for
another week or so.

Devin was pleased to hear that I was still pregnant,
but his mother was not. She hated my guts. She was not
going to let some little girl come and destroy her son's future
with an unwanted child.

One night that week, Devin called to say that he no
longer wanted the baby; that I had better have an abortion
because he was not ready for a child. I was devastated. *How
could he change his mind in a matter of days?* I wondered.
We had a big argument and a few days later I went through
with the abortion.

Both of our mothers had forbidden us to talk or see
each other. I was miserable. I was missing him like crazy
and the thought of not seeing him again made me feel sick.
Then one night when I was at my grandmother's house he
called, "Why are you calling here? You know we are not
supposed to be talking," I said.

"I know, I just wanted to see how you and the baby
were doing."

"What baby?" I asked.

"The one in your stomach," he answered.

"You mean you didn't know I had an abortion?"

"What? When did you do that?" Devin was furious.

"I had it done after you told me you didn't want the baby anymore. Don't you remember saying that to me?"

Devin paused for a moment then answered, "Yes I remember. But I only said it because my mom made me say it. I didn't think you were really going to do it."

"Well, I believed you so I went through with it. I wish I would have known you didn't mean it."

"So do I."

That night we talked on the phone until sunrise. I was so happy. I couldn't wait to see him again so the next day we hooked school and met at his house. It was like old times except we didn't have sex. We just talked about how much we missed each other and how happy we were to be together again.

Things were starting to get back to normal and my mother was doing much better. She had fewer trips to the hospital and my relationship with Devin was okay.

After a while, I started to notice other boys. For almost two years Devin had been the only person I was dating. But, no matter what I did or how hard I tried, I couldn't stop him from seeing other girls. I grew tired of his philandering and started to focus my attention elsewhere.

Kivey, an old childhood friend of mine, was transferred to my junior high school. Before long, we were inseparable. If you saw me, you were sure to see Kivey, and if you saw Kivey, I wasn't too far behind.

If I was wild, Kivey was savage. She was always into something. Whether it was reaping havoc in class or threatening to kick some poor innocent classmate's ass, Kivey was the baddest thing to hit Johnson Junior High School. Kivey plus Kerri equaled trouble and we knew it.

We hardly ever went to class. Practically every time we did we'd get our names put on the "Do Not Admit" sheet. It was a list of the names of students that had gotten into trouble and couldn't come back to the school until the principal had a conference with the student's parent. The security guard that patrolled the main entrance kept a copy of this list at his desk. My name made the list every other week.

Everyday I'd get into some kind of trouble at school. I had gotten expelled from school so much that my mother decided to transfer me to Walker Junior High.

Walker was a normal school with normal classrooms. My mother thought that by taking me away from Johnson, and the friends I had acquired there, that I would do better. Boy was she wrong. I didn't get expelled, but I continued to hook school. I found a new partner in crime and her name was Jada.

Jada and I would meet at school and conjure up a way to sneak out. We'd be sure to attend homeroom class just so that we'd be counted in the day's attendance. But, as soon as the first period bell sounded, we'd be on our way out the front door, the side door, or whichever door we could to hit the movies, go downtown, or to the mall. We practically lived at the mall.

Jada introduced me to this guy named A.J. After a few dates he claimed me as his girlfriend.

A.J. was about 6 feet tall and weighed over 250 pounds. Much to my amazement, he was in love with me. He would buy me anything I asked for, but I didn't like him as much as he liked me. I never had sex with him and can't even recall ever once kissing him, but he liked me anyway and went out of his way to please me.

One day Jada and I hooked school. We went to A.J.'s house to pick up some money he had promised me. After steady petition, A.J. agreed to give me $300 for a Gucci bag I had been eyeing, despite the fact that a few days before he had just given me $200 to buy a pair of oversized gold earrings with his name in them.

If he had a dime I wanted a nickel of it. He didn't have a problem with spending his money on me. He was a drug dealer and he knew that it was all part of the game.

Before A.J. gave me the money, he said that he was tired of always giving me money and not getting anything back in return. I told him that I wasn't ready to be intimate with him yet, but that someday I would.

I knew that if I didn't start putting out soon A.J. would stop giving me money so I promised that I would give him some of my teenage pussy when I got back from the Gucci Shop. Though I wanted to continue spending his money, I did not want to screw him. I was not attracted to him and the thought of letting his big ass climb on top of me made me want to hurl.

Reluctantly, he gave me the money, but only after I had promised to come back and sleep with him. I had absolutely no intentions of sleeping with A.J., let alone coming back to visit. I took the money and A.J. never saw me again.

CHAPTER THREE

Despite my mother's wishes, I continued to hook school and behave like a fool whenever I decided to attend class. I acted up in English class in particular. I was in Ms. Hanley's English class. Ms. Hanley was young, probably in her late twenties or early thirties. She dressed just as trendy as her ninth grade students. Her favorite outfit was a pair of black leather pants, a tight black shirt and those infamous purple, suede, thigh high boots. Never before had I seen a teacher dress like Ms. Hanley, which brings me to Trina.

Trina was a massive girl. She was about 6 feet tall with a medium build. Jada and I mostly hung out at school. Trina had her own set of school friends so we usually hung out after school. She reminded me of Kivey because she always had a bone to pick with somebody. Since she was so big she rarely had to actually fight anyone. Often times, all she would have to do is threaten someone and that would be enough for them to report her to the appropriate school authorities.

There was this one girl that Trina loved to torture. Everyday, Trina would call her names, follow her to the bus stop, and threaten to beat her up. The girl was so frightened that she would cry. She would beg Trina to leave her alone. She must have been really afraid because she never told anyone about it. Then Trina became bored with harassing her and found another girl to torment. This time it would be different.

Trina did the same thing to this girl. She called her names, followed her around the school and threatened to kick her ass. One day Trina, Jada and a few of our other friends were in the girls' bathroom. The new girl that Trina had been harassing walked in. She went into a stall and closed the door. Immediately, Trina started making fun of her, criticizing her clothes and hair. When the girl came out of the stall Trina jumped in her face and started to call her names. The girl tried to walk away, but Trina kept at it. The next thing we saw shocked the hell out of us. She pushed Trina to the other side of the bathroom and then beat the living daylights out of her. We couldn't believe it. Trina was getting her ass kicked right in front of us. We all died laughing.

Normally, no one could have gotten away with that. I am not the type to sit back and watch my friend get her ass kicked, but I swear she deserved it. She had no business bothering her because that girl never did anything to anyone. It was a lesson well learned for Trina. To this day, I still tease Trina about that day in the girls' bathroom.

I made lots of friends in junior high. High school was a whole other story. I changed schools so often that it was hard to develop friendships. And the fact that I had my own car, was well dressed in latest designer clothes and kept a man at my side didn't make matters any easier.

I lived and grew up in Southeast D.C. and wanted to meet people from other areas of the city, so I decided to attend a school in upper Northwest. The first high school I attended was Dulles Senior High.

Dulles had the same set-up as Johnson Junior High, it was an open-spaced school. On my first day at Dulles everyone was confusing me with a girl named Sheila. I would walk down the hall and people would mistakenly strike up a conversation with me until they realized that I wasn't Sheila. I had been hearing her name so much that day that I was dying to meet her. *Who the hell is Sheila and why is everybody mistaking me for her?* I wondered.

Later that day I met her. Now I knew why everyone was mistaking me for her. We looked just alike. We were both slim with creamy caramel complexions, chiseled facial features, and dressed in the same fashions. We instantly became friends.

Although I really liked Dulles, I was tired of traveling across town everyday so I was transferred to Manor Senior High School. Sheila and I remained friends even after I was transferred.

Manor was located in Northeast D.C. and was the closest high school to my neighborhood. Being at Manor was like being back in grade school. All my old buddies were there including Devin. It was his senior year and I was a sophomore. We had stopped dating for a while and I was distraught after learning that he had fathered a child by another girl who also attended Manor.

Despite his newfound fatherhood, I started seeing Devin again and soon he was expecting baby number two because I had gotten pregnant yet again. This time it was too late for an abortion. By the time I knew I had another bun in the oven I was nearly four months pregnant. *Here we go again* I thought to myself.

I tried my best to avoid my mother whenever possible. She was appalled. In the beginning of that pregnancy my mother did everything possible to try and get rid of me. She even tried to send me to St. Joseph's, which is a home for unwed teenage mothers.

The young mothers at St. Joseph's were usually homeless, in abusive relationships or abandoned by their parents. St. Joseph's afforded them a high school education, full-time childcare, and housing until they were stable. The downside was that they couldn't leave the premises without permission and could only have supervised visits with outsiders.

At first, St. Joseph's didn't seem like such a bad idea. Then I paid them a visit. After meeting the girls at the home my mind was made up. There was no way in hell I was going to live at a place that had as much freedom as a locked cell guarded by a starving pit bull. When my mother's attempt at St. Joseph's failed, she had no choice other than to accept the inevitable.

If that pregnancy didn't do anything else, it sure as hell made me think about some of the things I was into doing. I knew that if I wanted to graduate from high school and become somebody I had to at least start attending class regularly. So I did.

Soon, I attended class faithfully. One of my favorite classes at Manor Senior High was Health. Since I was about to give birth to a baby, learning about the human body and the female reproductive system was intriguing.

I almost never missed a day in Health class. I sometimes wonder what my life would be like if I never attended Manor. Before transferring there, Devin was the last thing on my mind. Manor is also the place where I met the person who would be the center of a lot of agony and confusion in my life, Joanne.

Joanne and I met in Health class. At first we would just talk in class and occasionally over the phone. One day we were casually talking about boys, school and the usual things that teenage girls talk about. Somehow we got off that subject and started to talk about our parents.

We discovered that our childhoods were about the same; both of our mothers were manic-depressives and that, for the most part, our fathers were absent. I was delighted to have someone to talk to who understood what I was going through with regards to my mother's illness. Most people didn't understand depression. Unfortunately I was forced to understand it. I had to deal with it everyday.

I was ashamed to tell people that my mother was sick. When she'd go away to the hospital and I'd have to stay with a relative I was afraid. I was afraid that people would think that she was crazy. I was afraid that she belonged in an insane asylum. I was afraid that she would kill herself and I'd become an orphan...a pregnant orphan. I was afraid that her sickness poisoned the blood in my veins, and that I would grow up to be just like her.

My fears would be overwhelming at times. I had watched my mother go from one extreme to the next. As long as she took her prescribed daily drugs she was fine. But whenever she tried to live without medication she'd turn into a different person. It seemed that every year, and often several times a year, she'd have nervous breakdowns. And each time her illness would progress to a different level.

Early on in my mother's illness she would simply become depressed and withdrawn. But in later years, she would hallucinate and take on schizophrenic-like behavior.

One day she really flipped out. She was having a nervous breakdown. I had tried to get in touch with my grandmother to see if someone could come over and help me calm her down.

When I was younger, my family would cater to my mother's every need whenever she got ill. Much to my mother's delight, that was then. I was now sixteen years old and she was no longer their problem, she was mine.

I was the only person she wanted to be around when she got sick. She didn't like for anyone else to see her in that condition, particularly her sisters. Besides, she had her teenage daughter to take care of her now.

Though it wasn't the first time I had seen my mother breakdown, it was one of the most frightening. She was hysterically crying, screaming, and cursing all at the same time. I was too afraid to go near her, but I couldn't just sit there and let her go crazy so I tried to calm her by talking to her. She didn't want to hear what I had to say. She cursed me out and told me to get out of her room. At that point I knew I had to do something so I called her doctor. He wasn't available so I called Sutton House, my mother had been a regular patient at the psychiatric ward there.

I told the doctor what was going on and asked if I could bring her in. He informed me that he could not force her to check-in and that I couldn't be the one to check her in either. She had to check-in herself.

"How in the hell is she supposed to check herself into the hospital if she is mentally ill and behaving like a stark raving lunatic?" I asked.

"Well, ma'am, that's the law. I don't know what else to tell you," he said before hanging up the phone.

I didn't know what to do. I talked to her and asked if she wanted to go to Sutton House. She said yes. She knew she was sick and needed help. She was usually willing to get treatment just as long as it wasn't at D.C.'s notoriously neglected, city operated, residential nut house, St. Mark's Hospital. She always had a fixating complex about St. Mark's and would surely perform if she had to go anywhere near that hospital.

I got her dressed and called a cab. I knew that she'd be there for at least a week or two so I was sure to pack a bag of clothes for her. As soon as we got in the cab she started rocking back and forth, talking to herself and laughing for no apparent reason. I was so embarrassed. The cab driver was looking at her through his rearview mirror trying to figure out what in the hell her problem was. Then he made a grave mistake, he got on the freeway.

Oh shit! What in the hell did he go and do that for I said to myself.

My mother was used to taking the long way to the hospital. When she realized the cab driver was headed for the freeway she became paranoid. She started to question him as to why he had taken the freeway and where he was taking us. She accused him of kidnapping and threatened to jump out the speeding car if he didn't get back on the main road. He was insulted and, before I knew it, they were bickering back and forth like two Ping-Pong balls. He was on the verge of throwing us out of his cab when I told my mother to shut up and leave him alone. He just looked at me and said, "God bless you child."

God must have blessed me. Otherwise I could not have endured all that I have and remained sane.

Minutes later we arrived at Sutton House. I thanked the driver and slipped him an extra ten dollars for the trouble. Since my mother didn't have health insurance she had two choices, Sutton House or St. Mark's, and you know she wasn't about to be going up in there. When we walked in everyone waved. She had been admitted to Sutton House so many times that she knew everyone there.

As far as treatment centers go, it was a nice place. She enjoyed the atmosphere there and usually got well fairly soon. However, even though it was separate from the actual hospital, Sutton House patients were required to be admitted via the hospital's emergency room. That didn't make any sense to me.

There was never a psychiatrist on duty at the main hospital and the doctor's that were there were ill equipped to handle my mother's sickness.

Contrary to the hospital's procedural policy, the doctors at the main hospital were capable of treating emergency injuries of the flesh, not of the mind.

A psychiatric nurse escorted us from Sutton House to the main hospital. Before my mother sat down she cursed everyone in the emergency room out and told them, "Don't be staring at me!" They all looked at her as if she had ten heads. No one was staring at her, at least not until she made herself noticeable.

When the doctor called her name we went back to the room where he was waiting. It wasn't an actual room with a door, rather simply a small section of the emergency room with privacy curtains surrounding a hospital bed.

He was a medical doctor, not a Ph.D. He did not know how to handle my mother's illness. He proceeded to ask her questions like, "So, tell me what's bothering you today?" Those were the types of questions that you would ask someone who was there for stomach pains, not mental anguish. After realizing that my mother wasn't playing with a full deck of cards, so to say, he called Sutton House to have someone from over there pick her up.

Before she was escorted back to Sutton House she would have to get some blood taken. My mother had always been needle phobic. She just couldn't fathom the idea of someone pushing that pointy little bastard in her arm so she started to perform again. "Oh no! Where do you think you are putting that thing?" she said to the doctor as he tried to draw her blood.

"Come on, it's not going to hurt. I just need to get a little blood from you so that we can make you all better."

"No, get that damn thing away from me."

"Please, I promise it won't hurt. I only need just a little drop."

I had never seen my mother so terrified.

"Stop or I'll punch you!" she screamed.

Needless to say, the only blood the doctor got was his own. My mother punched him in the nose and it took four people to get her off of him.

CHAPTER FOUR

A normal stay in the hospital for my mom was one week. She must have been really bad off because that time she would be there for over one month.

On one hand, I was sad for my mother and wanted her to get better so that she could come home. But on the other hand, I would have the apartment to myself and could do practically whatever I wanted. The thought of having absolutely no adult supervision was intriguing and if I could convince my mother to let Joanne stay while she was gone that would be even better. Joanne and I began to scheme on how we would approach asking.

First we went to visit my mother at Sutton House. I told her that I was afraid to stay in the apartment by myself and that since I was about five and a half months into my pregnancy I didn't want to be left alone. My mother said that she didn't mind if Joanne stayed just as long as she got permission from her mother. That was easy. Joanne's mother was sick of her anyway. So it was official, Joanne would stay with me until my mother came home.

We were ecstatic. Two high school girls home alone with no adult supervision, we had it made. Everyday was like a vacation. Summer was quickly approaching and we were having the time of our lives.

Although I was pregnant with Devin's child, we were playing relationship tag. One day we were together, the next day we hated each other's guts. I would meet different guys and go out on dates even as I was pregnant. Most of the guys didn't care. A couple of them even wanted me to leave Devin alone and start seeing them exclusively. Though I was flattered, I declined.
You would think that a pregnant girl couldn't get any play, but I swear I had more prospects then than I do now. It was an exciting time for me. Especially when my uncle Bug was released from prison.

Bug was my favorite uncle, but we weren't related by blood. He was the brother of my mother's old boyfriend, Trump, the guy who had played daddy to me. I hadn't seen Bug since I was about seven or 8-years-old. I just remembered him to be funny. He always made me laugh.
Back in the day Bug and Trump were big time drug dealers. They had it all; money, cars, designer gear and of course, women. Lots of women.

My mother dated Trump and was considered his main girl. He had several chicks on the side, a few of whom were my mother's so called friends. For years Trump lived the life of a hustler, but as fate would have it his luck eventually ran out.

Both Trump and Bug were arrested and sentenced to about 10 years each. Trump was to be released from prison first.

When Trump came out of jail he went back to doing what he knew best, dealing drugs. He was also into armed robbery. Before his arrest he was an accomplished bank robber and successfully took part in several jewelry heists.

Trump made one final attempt at a jewelry shop in suburban Maryland. Even with all his knowledge of heists, that last try would be fatal.

Trump and his right-hand man planned to rob the jewelry store. Apparently the plan was to have Trump do the actual theft and to have his partner drive the getaway car.

After a successful theft of the jewelry, Trump took the owner of the shop to the rear office, tied him up and left with the loot. The owner managed to free himself and followed Trump to his car where his partner was waiting. By the time Trump realized he was being followed by the shop owner it was too late. The store owner walked up to Trump's car and emptied his gun. Right there in broad daylight at a major street intersection he shot Trump and his partner to their deaths.

We were at my grandmother's house watching the news when the report came out. We didn't know it was Trump they were talking about. Even after seeing Trump's car on T.V., it still didn't register. We even commented on how foolish the robber was for not being certain that the owner was tied up good. Later that day we got the news that it was him.

My mother took Trump's death real hard. Even though they hadn't dated in years, he was her first love.

Bug was released from prison the following year. When he first saw me he hardly recognized me. I was all grown up and expecting a baby.

If Trump hadn't been killed he would have taken care of me just as if I was his own flesh and blood. He always had. He was the only father I knew. Before he was killed, we spent a lot of time together. He wanted to make up for all the years he had been in prison. Even though I wasn't his biological daughter, he took care of me. Bug knew that. And, since Trump was gone, Bug vowed to take his place.

Bug came out of jail with a new attitude. He had obtained a bachelor's degree in accounting while in prison. Although it was rare to have the chance to attend college courses while incarcerated, it was not impossible. He had simply hooked up with the right people in the right place at the right time.

While staying in a halfway house he found a job as an accounting clerk at a law firm. In less than six months he was promoted to accounting manager. His life had taken a turn for the better.

Over the course of the next year Bug and I would become inseparable. He was such an important part of my life that I couldn't go a day without seeing him.

He wasn't the best looking guy, but he had a heart of gold. He was one of the most down to earth people I have ever known. He would visit me everyday and take me anywhere I wanted to go. As long as he was having a good time, he was down with it. He was a true rebel without a cause.

Soon my mother would be released from the hospital, school would be back in session, and things would get back to normal. Joanne and I were getting used to life without parents and were not looking forward to my mother's return. When she came home she thanked Joanne for staying with me and sent her back home to her mother.

Joanne's mother had become accustomed to life without her so much that she sent her back home to my mother and Joanne ended up spending the next year at my house. We were both glad that her mother didn't want her to come back. Since we were both our mothers' only children, we didn't know what it was like to have siblings. She was the closest thing I had to a sister.

It was now September and school was back in session. I had changed schools yet again. This time I would attend Cambridge Senior High School.

After finding out about Cambridge's no-fee, onsite child care center, I quickly transferred. A new rule had gone into effect stating that students could only attend schools that were in their zone. Since Cambridge was not in my school zone, I had to petition for special permission to attend. Given the circumstances, permission was granted.

The childcare center was full to capacity and there

were about 20 or so people on a waiting list. But I wasn't worried. The baby wasn't due until late December and I had a plan that would surely get my baby into the next available slot.

I would make it a point to visit the center everyday. I became acquainted with all the girls and the babies, not to mention the center's director, Mrs. Jones.

Mrs. Jones was the type of person that could make you cry just by looking at you. Before I got to know her, I thought she was mean. She was always fussing at someone about something. The fact of the matter was that, she was not mean at all. She really loved the girls and babies in her program. She set the highest standards in her center and expected the young mothers to meet them. If they didn't they were kicked out of the program. It was just that simple.

Whenever the young mothers got off track, she would remind them of the many girls waiting to be in their shoes. She would tell them that there were plenty of girls who wished to be given the opportunity to finish school and know that their child was being well taken care of, all while not having to worry about money to pay for it.

Certain that it would secure my child's spot in the program, I told Mrs. Jones that I knew there were a lot of names on the waiting list, but that I couldn't afford to pay for childcare. I offered to help out around the center at lunch time and after school in exchange for my child's assurance in the program. She agreed. For the next three months I would do just that. And when it came time for me to return with my newborn baby, its spot would be guaranteed.

CHAPTER FIVE

My mother now had a full house. Devin had graduated from Manor and he too started to live with us. Joanne was in her senior year at Manor, while I was a junior at Cambridge.

Everyday Joanne would come home and brief me on the day's events and the latest gossip. On one day in particular, Joanne called me from a pay phone to tell me that she had just seen Janet driving a car with paper tags.

Janet was the mother of Devin's first child. Although he was a habitual liar and would deny that he was still seeing her, I knew better. Joanne didn't know for sure, but she suspected that Devin had bought the car for Janet. So did I. And I was determined to get to the bottom of it.

Later that day when Joanne came home from school, I questioned her. It was like a police interrogation.

"So, what kind of car was Janet driving?"

"It was a minivan. You know, a Mazda MPV."

"What color is it? Is it a cute car?" I asked.

"It's a minivan, it's cute for her."

"Who was riding with her? Was she by herself?"

"No. She was driving with a car full of girls, but I couldn't see who was in the car."

I was fired up. "How dare he go and buy that bitch a car when I'm six and a half months pregnant and ain't driving shit!" I screamed in disgust. I couldn't wait for him to come home so that I could curse his ass out.

As soon as he walked through the door, I started round two of my interrogation. He said that he did buy the car, but that it wasn't for her. He claimed he had bought the car as a second car, but that since his son's daycare was all the way on the other side of town, he had let Janet borrow the car so that she could get their son back and forth to daycare. After hearing his excuse I felt better.

Even at age 18, buying cars was no big deal for Devin. Back then he was a big time drug dealer. In those days D.C. was a drug dealer's paradise. Practically all the guys I knew were caked-up. Devin was pushing major quantities of cocaine and soon he was supplying the entire neighborhood with drugs.

Devin had hooked-up with a guy named Fuzzy. Fuzzy was from New York and had met Devin through a mutual friend. Devin had been selling drugs for years and always kept a nice stash. But Fuzzy took him to a whole new level. It wasn't unusual for me to help Devin count tens of thousands of dollars in cash. He trusted me with his money and soon he would trust me with everything.

At first Devin would only keep his money at my house. I didn't mind him stashing his money there. In fact, that was perfect. It meant that I had full access to it. Then, he started to keep his drugs there too. That was a big problem.

My mother didn't mind him keeping his money there either, but his drugs too? She would surely loose it if she found out. After a while, not only did I help him count his money, I helped him cook his drugs. We would be certain that my mother was at work whenever we cooked drugs in the house.

One day, Devin was in the kitchen *cooking*. It was about five o'clock and we had about another hour or so before my mother would be home from work. He told me to listen out for my mother and that if I heard her coming, to try to keep her from coming in the house. I did just that.

My mother had left work early that day and was on her way up the street when I spotted her. Devin was almost finished, but there was drug paraphernalia all over the place.

I rushed down the street to where my mother was standing and struck up a conversation with her. I told her that I wasn't feeling too well and needed some aspirin and asked if she could go to the store and get some while I went back in the house to lay down.

Normally my mother would have told me to go for myself, but I was pregnant and I guess she figured I just didn't feel like walking to the store. So she went to the store and by the time she walked in, Devin had finished and the kitchen was like new again.

Though Devin continued to stash his drugs at my place, that would be the last time I allowed him to cook it there. It was just a little too risky.

As my eventual delivery date grew closer, I started to have frequent doctor's visits. During the last few weeks of my pregnancy I would visit the Teen Center once a week. Devin had only went to a few doctor's visits with me. Even though I acted as if I didn't care whether he went or not, the truth is, I cared a great deal. I wanted him to be a part of the whole experience. It was new for me, and I was happy. I wanted him to share in my joy. When he showed little interest in being there for me, that made me feel worthless.

I had been a prenatal patient at the Southeast Teen Center. The teen center was popular among girls in the area. It was a place where teenaged girls could go for gynecological and prenatal check-ups, as well as sex education, parental counseling and birth control. As sad as it may be, those services were extremely needed in my neighborhood. The syndrome of babies having babies was far more complicated than a simple epidemic, it was a way of life. More than half of my childhood friends had given birth to babies before the age of eightteen, the other half had aborted them. So, it wasn't bizarre to see a girl in her teen years with a child in tow.

At times, I wonder if my life would be different had I not grown up in the inner city, if I had a father around, or better yet, if I had simply had a mother.

Many people will listen to me and say, "But you did have a mother." Yes, I had a mother in the theoretical sense, but not literally. My mother was too busy trying to be my best friend. She needed to be loved by someone so badly that she would give me anything I asked for. When my happiness was at stake the sky was the limit. Regardless of how unruly I had behaved or how many rules I had broken, my mother went out of her way to please me and rarely kept a punishment.

As a child, I would brag and boast about how much my mother loved me and would do anything for me. I was honored. But as I grew older, I began to see my mother's need for acceptance and approval as credulity and weakness, and ultimately the honor I once felt turned into mischief, then mischief turned into rebellion, and rebellion turned into flat out disrespect. Disrespect for my mother and eventually disrespect for myself.

It wasn't until recently that I realized how each and every experience I had endured as a child had a direct effect on my life as an adult. How my mother's choices in men were silently imbedded into my relationships. How my mother's need for acceptance and approval had rubbed off on me, and how my mother's illness had forced me to mature years ahead of schedule. It all made sense now. It was the cycle of life repeating itself and I was its star attraction.

CHAPTER SIX

Two weeks before my seventeenth birthday, and ten days overdue, the baby wasn't the least bit concerned with being born. I was extremely irritable and immensely horny. I was preparing to leave for a doctor's appointment when I heard Devin yell, "Hey Kerri, come here."

"I'm on my way out the door, what do you want?"

"Come back here and find out."

"Damn! What is it now?" I said to myself as I stomped back to the bedroom. When I opened the bedroom door Devin was lying on the bed naked.

"I know what will make you go into labor," he said in a sexy voice.

"What, castor oil?" I was being sarcastic.

"No, this will," he said while undressing me. He noticed how frustrated I was and felt that a good bump and grind would do the trick. In a matter of minutes I went from

Mrs. Attitude to Mrs. Gratitude. It was just what the doctored ordered.

Upon arriving at the teen center, I was informed that since I was so far overdue I would have to be transported to the hospital for an induced labor. I tried calling Devin at home but couldn't get an answer. I then called my mother, but she wasn't answering either so I went to the hospital alone in an ambulance.

Once at the hospital, I was able to reach Joanne who promised to let everyone in on the good news. Soon, Devin arrived with Joanne and my mother.

I had been given an IV with medication to contract the uterus. Devin was too spooked by the sight of blood, so he waited outside the delivery room until the coast was clear. Since I had been given an epidural and was completely oblivious to the pain, I didn't mind. My body was so numb that when the doctor told me to push, I couldn't tell whether I was pushing or pulling. After about ten minutes, I gave one push and the head appeared. The next and final push gave way to an eight pound baby girl. I was so relieved.

Joanne and my mother had been by my side during the delivery, while Devin's punk ass waited outside the door until he heard the baby's first cry. It was finally over. I now had the baby of my dreams and Devin and I would live happily ever after, or so I hoped.

The night I spent in the hospital was calming. Devin spent most of the day with me and the baby, but the hospital didn't allow visitors after 9 p.m. so he left and went home. He called me as soon as he got in and we talked on the phone all night long.

I was ecstatic. It was like we were meeting for the

first time and all of his attention was focused on me. I couldn't wait to see him the next day.

The following day my family came to visit. They began to ooh and ah over the precious little one and brought gifts for me and the baby. One of my aunts said that the baby looked like Devin's mother. Even though there was some resemblance, I didn't want to admit it. I still harbored ill feelings for her from years ago when she treated me so badly. Although we never had a good relationship and she desperately wanted me to disappear off the face of the earth, she loved her granddaughter. She came to visit the baby in the hospital and fell in love with her. She looked just like her.

I had already picked a name for the baby. Her name was going to be LaMaia. Devin and I argued for hours about that name. He insisted that since he was a so-called Muslim, our child would have an Islamic name. I had listened to about as much of his Islamic rhetoric as I could stand and agreed to give her an Islamic name, just as long as it was something I liked as well. We decided on Hasannah.

In the beginning of my parenthood, life wasn't so bad. Devin was spending a lot of time with Hasannah and me, and my mother was there to assist in any way possible. My mother would babysit whenever I needed, so I didn't miss out on much. I was still able to hang out with my friends and do practically everything that most teenagers did at that time. It was a lot easier than I had expected.

I stayed home with Hasannah for two months before returning to school. Mrs. Jones had promised me that

Hasannah could join the child care center when I returned to school, but she had expected me to return after six weeks. Since I stayed home for an additional three weeks, Hasannah's spot had been offered to another child and I had to find an alternative.

I didn't realize how expensive childcare was. Most of the centers I contacted quoted weekly rates in the one hundred dollar range for a child Hasannah's age. Since I didn't have a job, I looked elsewhere. Finally, an older woman who had babysat my cousin agreed to keep Hasannah. She charged half the price of the day care centers and had excellent references. Since she lived a few buildings down on the same street that I lived on, she was the ideal candidate.

When I returned to school it was like I had been transferred all over again. Since I had started attending Cambridge when I was pregnant, no one recognized me. All the boys were trying to get with me and the girls hated my guts.

After about two months, Mrs. Jones called to inform me that a spot had opened in the daycare and I could start bringing Hasannah to school with me. I was thrilled.

I enjoyed having Hasannah right there in school with me. I would eat lunch in the daycare center and check on her periodically throughout the day. The only downside was that it was the middle of winter and I didn't like the fact that I had to catch the bus to school with her in the cold. Fortunately, that only lasted about two weeks.

Everyday I would come home and complain about my having to catch the bus with the baby half way across town in the freezing cold. Devin grew sick of my wining and complaining so he went out and bought me a car. It was my first car and I loved it.

Now that I had a car the girls at my school really hated me. I made two or three female friends, while most of my friends at school were boys. One day I was on my way to class when I ran into a girl I had met in the child care center. Her name was Lisa.

Lisa didn't have a baby, but her God-daughter was in the school's child care center and she would eat lunch with us sometimes.

She asked if I could give her a ride to the store. Since Hasannah was not at school with me that day, I said okay.

We never did make it back to school. We spent the rest of the day driving around and shopping. I had made a new friend.

The next day Lisa introduced me to some of her friends and soon we all became friends. Each day at lunch time we would meet in the cafeteria and gossip for the first half hour, the second half hour was spent in the daycare with the kids.

As my social life was getting better at school, at home it was deteriorating. Devin was becoming more and more distant and we didn't spend as much time together. I started to suspect he was cheating. At first I had no hard evidence. He would show the usual signs of a cheater like taking too long to answer my pages, not returning my phone calls, and coming home late or sometimes not at all. We were still living with my mother and it was like he didn't live there anymore. The only time I saw him was when I woke up in the morning, and that was on a good day.

I knew he was cheating, but with whom? I didn't have the slightest idea. It could have been anyone. Since he was cute and had a lot of money all the girls were after him, but I was determined to keep him for myself.

When I started to suspect he was cheating, I started seeing other people. For a while I wouldn't even think about cheating on him. I was in love. But when I realized that he was cheating on me, I said to myself, "Two can play that game," and so I did.

I now realize that I should have just left him alone, but back then I didn't see it that way. I thought that if we split up it would have proven everyone right that said it never really was going to work out; that he really didn't love me as much as he said he did. Everyone warned me of what would happen. They said that when young girls have babies by young men, more often than not, the girls are left to raise children alone. They said that as soon as the babies are born the fathers mysteriously disappear. That is what I was told, but I refused to listen. In my mind that was not my destiny. Devin loved me and our child and we were destined to be together forever. In my mind, Devin was my destiny.

Devin decided that it was time for him to move out. The only problem was that he didn't have a legal occupation and could not qualify for an apartment. So I talked to Uncle Bug about signing for an apartment for him. Since he and Devin had become good friends and Devin was supplying the drugs Bug was selling as a side gig, Bug didn't mind. Shortly thereafter, Devin moved into a luxury apartment in the suburbs. Although we were both seeing other people, we continued to see each other on occasion.

When Devin moved out things at home started to go

haywire. Joanne and I were drifting further apart and my mother was trippin'. We would argue about the most senseless things. Everyday was a struggle. One day my mom and I had a big argument and she told me to leave. She said that she was sick of my shit and she wanted me to get out of her house. I was just as sick of her shit as she was of mine so I left.

I called Devin and told him what had happened and asked if the baby and I could stay with him. He said yes and the next day I moved in.

Initially, we had agreed that we would continue to see other people and that we would live together as roommates. That lasted all of one day. Devin demanded that I stop seeing other guys. He didn't want me to do anything more than go to school and come straight home. That would have been okay by me if he had agreed to do the same, but he didn't. He continued to see other girls and came home late every night. He would deny that he was with someone else and offered his usual "In this line of business, you have to be out late at night to get your money" excuse as to why he didn't get home until the break of dawn. I knew he was cheating and vowed that if I ever caught him I would leave him for good.

Each day was about the same. I woke up at 5:30 am allowing enough time to get myself and the baby dressed and drove the 35 mile trek from our apartment in Upper Marlboro, Maryland to Cambridge High School in upper Northwest D.C. At three o'clock I would go straight home, cook dinner, clean the house and wait for Devin to arrive, which was usually well after midnight.

Most of the time he wanted sex as soon as he walked through the door. If I was in the mood, he'd get what he wanted. However, during that time, I wasn't interested in sex. What I needed was love and support and I wasn't getting either from him. I was fed up with him and was planning to leave when I received the news I had been waiting for.

Tamera, one of my oldest childhood friends, had called. I hadn't talked to her in a while and was pleased to hear her voice. I knew that something must have been wrong because we didn't talk often. For her to have called it must have been important.

Before she broke the news to me she made me promise that I wouldn't tell Devin that she was the person who told. I assured her that I wouldn't mention her name, then she spilled her guts. She told me that she knew whom Devin was cheating on me with. It was Marie, and that was just the beginning. She said that not only was Marie sneaking around with Devin, but that Joanne was in on it.

Joanne knew what was going on the whole time, but never said a word. Tamera said that just two days prior to her telephone call, Marie, along with Joanne and two of their other friends, went to Manor High School's senior prom in Devin's car.

I was shattered. I became so brain-numb that I didn't hear anything else Tamera said. Paralyzed with rage, I couldn't believe what I was hearing. It wasn't the fact that Devin was cheating that hurt so bad, it was the fact that Joanne, my best friend, my confidant, my sister, knew about it all along. She knew that I was head over hills in love with Devin and she never said a word to me about what was going on. I was frantic.

After talking to Tamera I went into a state of deep depression. I didn't know which way to turn. Here I was, 17-years-old, with a baby and a good for nothing, poor ass excuse for a man. What was I to do? I couldn't go back home to my mother, she didn't want me anymore. I was too ashamed to go to my grandmother, so I just stayed put. I pretended that I didn't know about Marie and stayed with my good for nothing, trifling ass baby's daddy.

That summer was a hard time for me. It was a time of regrouping and rebuilding my own self-worth. I had decided that I wasn't going to let mere mortals dictate my degree of happiness. Vowing to rid myself of all negative people and things, I shut off all communication with Devin and Joanne.

In an effort to get my life back in order I went back home to live with my mother. Since there was no one else around our relationship grew stronger than ever.

With Devin away, my financial status was practically non-existent. I was always down to my last penny and constantly borrowing money from people. Eventually I got a job at a local drug store.

I had always kept a job. My first job was at a shoe store. That only lasted two weeks because they found out that I was only fourteen. After that I worked several jobs in the retail industry until I graduated from high school.

Working was second nature to me. While most teenage girls in my shoes would have probably gotten on welfare, it was never a thought in my mind. I never applied for welfare, food stamps or any other program offered by the government. I saw them as a trap. Besides, I had several marketable skills and could earn more money working part-time gigs than collecting welfare checks.

While the money I was making was consistent, it wasn't much, just six or seven dollars per hour at the most. I was so used to shopping whenever I wanted and buying things without checking the price tag that I became extremely frustrated when I couldn't do it any longer. Going from dealing with a big time drug dealer and having access to hundreds of dollars a day to making minimum wage was arduous. I set out on a mission to find an unsuspecting suitor to help make ends meet.

A friend of mine was having a dance or cabaret as we called it. I hadn't been out dancing in a while so I decided to go. When I arrived, the place was jammed pack. The D.J. was pumping and everyone was having a good time. I started dancing as soon as I hit the door. After dancing to two or three songs I needed to take a break so I went to sit with a table of friends. While I was sitting this guy asked me to dance.

The first thing I do when a guy approaches me is look at his shoes and then his teeth. If his shoes and teeth are in order I check everything in between.

His shoes were okay and so were his teeth so I said yes. He wasn't the best looking guy nor was he a good dancer, but he was polite. He didn't approach me in the usual vulgar manner that most men do, he was a gentlemen. That goes a long way with me. The fact that he was so polite and well mannered overshadowed the fact that he was, to put it mildly, butt ugly.

He followed me around the whole night until finally

we exchanged numbers. I promised to call him the next day, but he beat me to it and called me about 8:00 that morning. I thought he must have been crazy because I didn't get in until after 4:00 am and I was tired as shit. I talked to him for a few minutes then went back to sleep.

Later that day he called again. He asked if I wanted to go out to dinner, but I didn't know if I wanted to be bothered with him. He seemed a little desperate. There's nothing worse than a man who will not take no for an answer.

I told him that I would call him later with an answer, but he insisted that he see me. Since I didn't have anything else planned, I said yes. He arrived on time as scheduled. "Ooh, prompt and polite. I just might start liking this guy after all," I said to myself.

His name was Ronnie. He was 25-years-old and I was 17. We hit it off right from the start. At first, I was only interested in a platonic relationship with Ronnie. Then, after spending some time together I grew to like him. He was almost perfect. Just as I required in every relationship before him, he took care of me. Whatever I wanted, Ronnie would see to it that I got it. Never mind the fact that he still lived at home with his grandmother, and who cared that he didn't have a car or a job? None of that mattered to me. What did matter was that he gave me everything I asked for.

Ronnie had a good excuse for not having a job. Let him tell it, he couldn't work because of his injury. Approximately one year before I met Ronnie, he had been stabbed several times in the back while attending a popular nightclub. Though his injury was real and he did bear visual scars, he still could have held a job. He had hired an attorney and sued the nightclub based on the fact that there were metal detectors at the door and the person who stabbed him had managed to get past them. He went to trial and won the case. The judge ordered the nightclub to pay him punitive damages in excess of over $300,000, but Ronnie would never see a dime of that money. The nightclub appealed the judge's decision and began an ongoing battle. Ronnie was so infatuated with the thought of getting this lump sum of money that he had practically given up on working and was waiting patiently for the check to show up in the mail.

We had a sort of don't ask, don't tell relationship. I never asked him where he was getting money from and he never told me. All I know is that if I asked Ronnie to buy me something on Monday, by Tuesday it was in my possession. To me that was all that mattered.

After a few months of being with Ronnie exclusively I was not happy. He was taking care of me and 9-month-old Hasannah, but I was getting sick of him. I wasn't physically attracted to him and I'd started feeling bad because I was using him.

Ronnie was such a nice person, just not the one for me. When I tried to explain how I felt he would break down. He was in love with me and couldn't understand why I didn't want to be with him. Every time I tried to leave him he would show up with lavish gifts. He would send me flowers and would call my mother and try to get her to help him get me back. It was ridiculous.

He would call me fifty times a day and leave fifty desperate messages on my answering machine. I mean he would just do whatever it took to win me over. After a while, I stopped trying to leave him and eventually started cheating on him.

By this time, I was 18-years-old, a year had passed and I was still with Ronnie. Still living at home with my mother, I was now in my senior year of high school.

One day I had gotten some money from Ronnie to buy an outfit I saw at the mall. When I returned from the mall Jamillah had called to ask me for a favor. She had just come from seeing a car for sale. It was only 500 bucks and she was dead broke. She desperately wanted this car and wanted to know if I had any money to loan her, but I had just spent $400 on an outfit and a watch.

Even though I had just started hanging out with Jamillah and we were not very close at the time, I sympathized with her need for transportation. I told her that I would take the stuff I had just purchased back for a refund if she could pay me back within a few weeks. She was ecstatic.

The next day I took the merchandise back and gave the money to Jamillah. She was so grateful that she promised to get me the exact same outfit along with anything else I wanted.

CHAPTER SEVEN

When you grow up in the ghetto, you must have a scheme. If you don't learn anything else, you'll surely learn how to run a hustle. There are so many hustles in the ghetto. Some people sell drugs, some steal cars, some rob banks, some commit financial crimes such as check fraud and credit card scams while others boost.

When Jamillah told me that she was a booster, I didn't believe her. She didn't fit the profile. Most boosters steal with the intention to sell the merchandise for a profit. She didn't. She stole with the intention to save her money. The next day she would prove that she was in fact, a booster, and a damn good one at that.

Jamillah and I went to the mall so that she could steal the merchandise I had just returned. I couldn't believe how easy it was to steal from such high security department stores. When we went to the car, she showed me what she had gotten away with. I was flabbergasted. Not only did she get the same exact outfit I had just returned, but she also got the watch and a pair of shoes.

"How did you get the security alarm tags off the clothes?" I asked in disbelief.

"I popped them off," she replied.

"How?"

"I can't explain it, I'll have to show you." Jamillah was nonchalant about the act.

In less than one hour, she had went into a major upscale department store with security cameras all over the place and security alarm tags attached to the merchandise, and came out with over $500 worth of goods without spending one red cent.

That would be my first experience with boosting, but it surely wasn't my last. I began accompanying Jamillah to the mall almost everyday and each day we'd leave with a trunk full of goodies.

In the beginning, Jamillah would steal everything for me. I was just a tag-along. Eventually, she grew tired of stealing for me and told me to learn how to steal my own stuff. She was so busy stealing for the two of us that she couldn't get the things she really wanted for herself.

At first I was too afraid to steal. I thought that she was just saying that because she was mad about not being able to get one particular outfit. But when I realized she was serious, my mind was made up. I knew that if I wanted to continue to get things without paying for them I would have to steal my own stuff. And so I did. Before long, I was going to the mall each and everyday stealing anything that wasn't nailed down. I had become a booster.

When Ronnie found out I was stealing he was furious. "You don't have to be no thief. I give you everything you want!" he would say.

It was the truth. I didn't have to boost, I simply wanted to. When I discovered how easy it was I became addicted. Ronnie would give me money to go shopping. Instead of spending my money at the mall, I'd steal whatever I wanted. It was a glorious scheme until I got caught.

One day I had went to the mall with Jamillah and her sister. By this time I had been stealing for months and considered myself a professional kleptomaniac. I had gotten away with tens of thousands of dollars in clothes and shoes and was confident that I would leave the store with more trinkets to add to my collection. As usual, we split up when we went inside the store. This technique was key because store clerks were more suspicious of three young black girls shopping together as opposed to us shopping alone.

Whenever we'd go stealing, we'd be sure to wear our best outfits. I would only steal upscale designer name brands. A typical outfit would retail for $250 at the very least. There would be days when I'd leave one upscale department store with thousands of dollars worth of merchandise in one boost.

Just like before, I had big plans for this boosting session. But so did the undercover security guards. They had been watching me from the moment I walked into the store.

I went to the section of the store that housed the particular designer I liked. I didn't see much that I was interested in, but one outfit did catch my eye. I took it in the dressing room and popped the alarm tag off, stuffed it in my purse and headed for the door.

Whenever I had stolen an outfit and was near the exit door, I would always get paranoid. I would feel like everybody was watching me. Suspicious of anyone giving me direct eye contact, I would scan the isles of the store looking for anyone wearing a rugby shirt and khaki pants.

I don't know why, but for some reason people who work undercover for department store security always wear rugbies and khakis. Maybe it's because they're trying to blend in, but usually it doesn't make them blend in, it actually makes them stand out, especially when you're dealing with the caliber of stores I frequented.

As I headed for the exit doors I started to feel paranoid again. I was looking around trying to spot anyone who looked suspicious. By the time I realized that an undercover security guard was behind me it was too late.

Too late to empty my purse, too late to put the outfit back on the shelf, I just kept walking. There was about 10 feet between the undercover and me and about 10 feet between me and the door. I sure as hell wasn't going in the direction of the undercover so I just walked out the door.

For a moment I thought I had gotten away. I thought that maybe he was just a normal customer who was fond of rugbies and khakis, but my first instinct was correct. As soon as I walked out the door, he walked up behind me and grabbed my arm. He flashed a special police badge and told me to go with him. I knew that if I had tried to run, Montgomery County police would have put out an All Points Bulletin. Besides, there was no need for me to run. The outfit was under $200 and I knew that I would be charged with a misdemeanor.

As I was walking with the security guard to the back of the store, I was thinking all sorts of things. *What if they lock me up and throw away the key? Ronnie is going to kill me when he finds out. I'm not telling these motherfuckers shit.* I was trying to get my story together in my head before the security guard started to question me.

Before I ever started boosting, I was told what to say and do if I ever got caught.

Just as I had expected, the security guard started asking questions. He handcuffed me to a bench, took a headshot picture of me, and started his examination. The first question he asked was did I come alone or with someone else. I told him that I came alone. He then asked me how did I get the alarm tag off the clothes. I told him that there wasn't one on that particular outfit and that was the reason I had picked it. He asked why I had stolen the outfit. I told him that I had a child who needed pampers and milk and I didn't have any money. I said that I had planned to steal the outfit and sell it for half price. I don't know whether he believed my story or not, but he must have felt sorry for me because he wasn't interested in pressing charges.

Almost off the hook, a female security guard walked in and flipped the script. She wasn't interested in hearing anything I had to say. She hated thieves and if it were up to her, she'd have me put away for life.

The male security guard tried to convince her to let me go, but she was determined not to let me get away. She called the police and I was hauled off to jail.

When I arrived at the precinct, I was allowed one telephone call. I called Ronnie. I told him what had happened and asked him to come and bail me out. "See...I told you so...what were you thinking?" Ronnie was livid.

The commissioner set my bond at $200. Since I didn't have a previous record, I was released on my own recognizance. By the time Ronnie got there, I was waiting outside the police station.

It was a long ride home. In actuality it only took about 20 minutes, but with Ronnie's ranting and raving it seemed like hours. By the time we got to my mother's house it was almost midnight. Hasannah was fast asleep. I asked Ronnie not to tell my mother what happened and he agreed.

Although I was still with Ronnie, I had started seeing Devin again. I wasn't in love with Devin anymore, I was just on a mission.

While we were apart, Devin had gotten another girl pregnant. It was Marie, the friend of Joanne who Devin had been cheating on me with. I wasn't surprised to learn that she was pregnant. She was desperate for attention and determined to make Devin her man.

When I learned that Marie was pregnant, I was determined to make her miserable. She was the reason I had ended my relationship with Devin. I didn't really want to be with him, I just wanted to make Marie jealous.

Ronnie began to suspect that I wasn't faithful. Everyday he would ask me if I was cheating on him and I'd tell him what he wanted to hear. Even though I denied it, he knew I was seeing someone else. He was in denial. After a while, I couldn't bear cheating on him so I just left him alone. He was distraught.

Marie was in her third trimester of pregnancy. Devin had all but forgotten about her and started to see me again. The day that Marie had her baby I was at Devin's house. I was on the telephone talking when the other line clicked. I told the person I was talking to, to hold on, that there was another call waiting. I answered the other line. The voice on the other end asked, "Is Devin there?"

"Who is this?" I asked.

"This is Marie, who is this?"

"Don't worry about it," I teased.

"Is this Kerri?" Marie asked.

I just hung up the phone.

Marie called right back. Once again, she asked to speak to Devin, but this time her tone was nastier, "Put Devin on the phone, bitch!"

I replied, "Fuck you," and hung up the phone.

The next time Marie called, she dished an arsenal of insults and threatened that when she caught me, she was going to kick my disrespectful ass.

A couple of months later, Jamillah and I were en route to the Galleria at Tyson's Corner Mall to do some light boosting. As we exited the shortcut through Fort Dupont Park, we heard a loud crash.

"What was that?" asked Jamillah.

I turned around and looked out the back window. "Damn, the two cars behind us just had an accident," I said nonchalantly. I was about to check my lipstick in the sunvisor mirror when Marie came dashing around the corner.

She had noticed Jamillah's car and in an effort to catch up with us, Marie rammed her car into the back of someone's vehicle. She was so desperate to "kick my disrespectful ass" that she didn't even get out of her car at the scene of the accident, she simply kept driving in our direction.

"Pull over Jamillah, I'mma kick that bitch ass!" Marie yelled while driving parallel to Jamillah's car.

Jamillah turned to me and asked if I wanted her to pull over.

"Girl, fuck Marie. I don't have time for this shit. We have the kids in the back seat and, furthermore, I'm trynna make it to Neimen Marcus before they close."

"Are you sure you don't want me to pull over?" Jamilla asked.

"I'm sure. Besides, why fight someone I know I can beat anyway?"

"True that," Jamillah said. She then switched into the left lane. We were headed for the Sousa Bridge just before the Southeast-Southwest Freeway when Jamillah said, "Oh my God! Kerri, you aint gonna believe this shit. That bitch is following us!"

I looked to see for myself. "Yep! She sure is!"

"Are you sure you don't want me to pull over? This bitch needs to get her ass kicked!" Jamillah was fired up.

"Girl, no. I'm not trippin' off Marie, I'm trynna get to Neimen's. Shit, they close in two hours and this traffic aint no joke."

Jamillah proceeded with the original plan and kept driving. By this time, we were on the little stretch of road by the Potomac River, just before the Virginia Avenue and Route 66 West split. Then, just as Jamillah was about to take the exit towards Route 66, Marie zoomed up behind us and started honking her horn, motioning for Jamillah to pull over.

"Okay, Kerri. This is getting to be ridiculous. This bitch is gonna keep following us until we stop so you might as well get out and kick her ass!" Jamillah was persistent.

"Okay, okay. I didn't want to fight her at first, but fuck it. She deserves a beat down. It's one thing to threaten to kick my ass, but it's a whole 'nother thing to make me miss that banging ass outfit I spotted at Neimen's!"

I didn't know what had gotten into Marie. Maybe
Devin had pumped her head up so much that she really
thought she was the shit, or maybe the two girls that were
riding with her foolishly gave her far too much over-
exaggerated confidence. But for whatever reason, Marie was
determined to make Jamillah pull over so that she could kick
my disrespectful ass.

Jamillah drove into an empty parking lot just off the
freeway and Marie pulled up right behind her.
Before we got out of the car I told Jamillah to make
sure that the two girls that were with Marie, the same two
girls that had went to the prom with Joanne and Marie in
Devin's car, didn't try to jump in. I also told her under no
circumstances should any of them try to break up the fight.

We all jumped out of the two cars simultaneously. I
went straight for Marie. Before she could even lift a finger, I
grabbed a handful of her long hair, bent her over face-down,
and showered her with uppercuts to the head.
Marie was screaming for me to let her go, but I
couldn't. She had talked so much shit and threatened me so
much that I just couldn't let her get off that easily. I threw
her trash talking ass to the ground and with my brand
spanking new high heeled Via Spiga boots, stomped her
weightless body into the pavement like the no-count ghetto
superstar that she was. As I hovered over Marie stomping
her body like a project roach, I felt something hit me upside
the head.
Jamillah went to check on the kids in the car and
while she wasn't looking, one of the girls that was riding
with Marie snuck in and hit me in the head with a diaper bag.

I left Marie lying on the ground for dead and charged for the girl who had snuck in a hit, but she was lucky. I took one look at her 8-month pregnant belly and warned, "Bitch, you are lucky to be pregnant, or else I would kick your fucking ass! But when you have that baby your ass is mine!"

And just like that, it was over. I looked both of Marie's friends up and down from head to toe, spit on Marie's motionless body and told Jamillah, "Come on, if we hurry we can catch Neimen's before they close."

As we were about to get into the car, Jamillah looked back and noticed that the two girls were trying to lift Marie up off the ground. Jamillah and Marie's aunt, Natifah, were good friends. Though Jamillah was on my side and encouraged me to kick Marie's ass, she wanted to make sure that Marie was still breathing.

Marie was lying on the ground face-down and immobile. I had her blood all over my clothing and there were strands of her hair still wrapped around my fingers.

Jamillah got out of the car and asked Marie if she was okay. Marie didn't answer, so Jamillah walked over to see what was going on.

Marie's face was banged up. She had knots on her forehead, her nose was busted and her mouth was bleeding. Her eyes were so puffy that her eyeballs were barely visible.

Jamillah took one look at Marie and told her that she had no business trying to fight me and that she didn't feel sorry for her and that she got exactly what she deserved.

As Marie's friends loaded her battered body into the back seat of her car, Jamillah told them, "She needs to see a doctor, take her to the hospital. Columbia Hospital for Women is right down the street." And with that, Jamillah got back into the car and we drove off.

Though we had ample time to make it to the mall, we decided to go back around the way instead. We were both so giddy about what had just taken place that we had to spread the news right away.

The first stop we made was at Jamillah's sister's house. As soon as she opened the door she started with the questions, "Damn Kerri, why you got blood all on your clothes and shit? What y'all been up to?"

Jamillah butted in. "Chile, let me tell you what just happened. We were on our way to the mall . . ." and Jamillah told it like it was.

We stayed at Jamillah's sister's house and laughed at Marie for hours.

I knew that my mother would get a kick out of the story so I called home to fill her in. "Hi Ma, what's up?"

"Nothing, just got finished kicking Natifah's ass," she said matter of factly.

"Natifah?" I was puzzled.

"Yeah, I kicked that bitch ass."

"When? What happened?"

"She and two other girls came up here talking 'bout they were looking for you. I asked her what they were looking for you for and she said because you and Jamillah had jumped her niece Marie and that she was going to fuck you up when she caught you. Girl, you know your mamma don't play that shit, so I opened the door and punched that bitch in the face."

"Ohmigod! You did what?" I couldn't believe what my mother was telling me.

"That's right. I punched that big bitch in the face I told her she wasn't gonna do a damn thing to my baby."

"When did this happen?"

"About fifteen minutes ago."

"Where is she now?"

"I don't know, the girls that were with her broke the fight up and they left."

"Wait a minute . . . so what happened, are you okay?"

"I'm fine, but I didn't have any clothes on." She snickered as she recounted the story, "Yeah girl, she picked the right one. I had just gotten out of the shower when they started banging on the goddamn door. I was so mad, I forgot I didn't have any clothes on. I opened the door in my bra and drawers and punched that bitch dead in her mouth! That'll teach that bitch about knocking on people's doors and shit! I bet she won't try that trick no more."

I laughed at the thought of my mother on the porch in her bra and panties, let alone the thought of her fighting big ass Natifah all by herself. My mother was about 5'2" and Natifah was 6 feet tall or better, so you can just about imagine how ridiculous that must have looked.

I told my mother not to open the door if they came back and that I was on my way home. On the way over to my house I started thinking about what my mother had said.

"Jamillah, Marie must have told Natifah that me and you jumped her."

"Come on now Kerri, what we look like jumping her little ass?" Jamillah was insulted.

"Girl, she crazy! I know she ain't go home and tell people we jumped her! It was two of us and three of them, so how in the hell could we have jumped her?"

Jamillah looked at me and laughed. "Never mind that. Why in the hell would I have jumped in the fight anyway? You were kicking her ass so bad I didn't need to jump in. If anything, her friends needed to jump in and help her punk ass out!"

Before we went to my place I made a stop at Trina's house. Trina and I had remained good buddies since my days at Walker Junior High. I knew she would be down with kicking some ass.

My mother must have seen us drive into the parking lot because as soon as we parked, she came running outside. We all went back inside the house and she started telling us what had happened.

I took a good look at my mother and noticed that she had a small knot on her forehead.

"Ma…what happened to your head? Did Natifah put that knot on your head?" I was pissed.

"It must have happened when we were fighting, but don't worry Kerri, I kicked her ass!"

That was all I needed to see. I jumped up and said, "I'll be damned if this bitch is gonna come up here putting knots and shit on my mother's head!" I went into the kitchen and grabbed the longest, sharpest knife I could find.

I told Jamillah and Trina to follow me, that we were going to find Natifah and I was going to kill that bitch.

As Jamillah and Trina were trying to talk some sense into me, I ran out the back door. We jumped in Jamillah's car and just as we were exiting the parking lot, Natifah and a car full of girls were entering the parking lot.

Both cars stopped and we all jumped out at the same exact time.

I gripped my knife as tight as I could and charged full speed toward Natifah, "Bitch, I'mma kill you!"

Natifah saw the knife in my hand and began to run in the opposite direction. I chased her to the other side of the complex.

She was running faster than Marion Jones and I was hot on her heels. She kept yelling, "Put the knife down, put the knife down, if you wanna fight, we can fight, just put the knife down!"

"Bitch fuck you! I'm not puttin' shit down!" I said as I lunged for a piece of her flesh.

Natifah ran so fast and jumped so high that I couldn't get to her. I was pissed. I wanted to kill that bitch right there on Alabama Avenue.

She had crossed the line. It was one thing to verbally harass me, but to come to my house so-called looking for me, ooh that bitch was gonna get it!

Finally, I got close enough to her to slash a piece of her skin with the tip of the knife. I was blown. I wanted my knife to carve a chunk of her meat like a Butterball turkey on Thanksgiving Day.

Then she tried to grab the knife from me. At that point everyone that was outside closed in on us and tried to break the fight up before someone got hurt. The next thing I knew, Natifah and her friends were running to their cars trying their best to get out of Dodge.

If nothing else, I succeeded in making Marie jealous. And to add insult to injury, I whipped her ass as well. After that incident I was through with Devin for good.

Even though I had left Ronnie alone, he was still hanging on. He would call daily just to check on me. Eventually, I gave in and started to see him again. He was enamored.

With all that had been going on, school was the last thing on my mind. Graduation was only weeks away and I wasn't sure whether or not I would walk across the stage.

After coming home from school one day I had decided to take a walk to the store. As I was walking, I started to think about my Uncle Bug. I hadn't seen him in a few days and was eager to fill him in on all the madness that had been going on.

I was on my way back from the store when an old friend saw me walking. He pulled over and asked if I wanted a ride. I said yes and got in the car.

We were casually talking when he said, "That's fucked up what happened to Bug."

"Bug who?" I asked in a frazzled voice.

"Trump's brother."

When I realized he was talking about my Uncle Bug, my heart nearly dropped to my stomach.

"What? What happened to Bug?" I asked frantically.

"Damn, you didn't know?"

"No! Know what!"

"They found him outside of his apartment building. Somebody shot him in the back three times. He's dead."

For a minute I was so stunned that I couldn't even think straight.

"Kerri, are you okay?" my friend asked.

I sat there in a hopeless daze, oblivious to my surroundings. I heard him talking to me, but I couldn't answer.

"Hey shorty, you aight?"

"I think I'm gonna be sick."

I was overcome with sadness. The tears scurried down my face like fifteen-pound bowling balls. My head felt cloudy and my heart was heavy. I felt as if someone had just reached inside my chest, ripped my heart out and sliced it into a billion little pieces.

I didn't even realize I was in front of my apartment building until he said, "Kerri, you aight? You need me to help you with your bags?"

I jumped out of the car, ran into the house and called Bug. His answering machine picked up, "Hi, this is Bug, I'm not in right now. Please leave a message after the beep."

"Bug, it's me! If you're in there, pick up. It's me! Please pick up the phone. Please call me! Please! God help me!"

I completely lost it. I ran in my mother's room and told her what had happened. She too started to cry. We both sat there in her room and cried like babies.

Although I knew it was true, I didn't want to accept it. I wanted to believe that he was okay, that it was just a terrible rumor. I wanted to believe that Bug was still alive. Maybe he went away for the weekend or maybe he just wasn't picking up the phone. I was willing to accept anything but him being dead.

I continued to call him every hour on the hour and paged him repeatedly. I told my mother not to worry, that he was okay and that he would be calling me any minute now. I told her that when he called we were going to go out to eat or clubbing, just as he used to do with Joanne and me.

For hours I sat by the phone unable to move, waiting for a call that would never come.

CHAPTER EIGHT

When Bug died I had lost my best friend. I had never been through anything like that before. I had so much love and respect for him; he was the closest thing I had to a father after Trump died. It seemed as if I was cursed. It seemed that whenever things would start to look up, there would be an unforeseen downfall lurking in the midst.

I didn't even get the chance to pay my last respects. It was the end of the school year and final exams were being taken. My English teacher informed me that if I missed the final exam I would not graduate because they were not offering make-up exams. I was distressed. The final exam was being held on the same day as Bug's funeral. I would have to choose between Bug's funeral and graduating.

I loved Bug dearly, but I wasn't about to let twelve years of schooling go down the drain. So, instead of attending his funeral, I went to school ready to be tested.

As I waited for the instructor to pass out the exam, I cried. I circled in the answers with my yellow no. 2 pencil and cried even harder. I just kept thinking about my uncle and picturing his lifeless body propped up in a casket. It was overwhelming. The tears were streaming down my face as I fled the exam room. I just couldn't take it. How could I concentrate on the test when the funeral director was probably reading his obituary?

In my head I pictured the whole scene. I could see hundreds of mourners. I could see him lying there. I could hear the organ playing "Precious Lord." I could hear the choir singing "It's so hard to say goodbye." I could hear his girlfriend crying as the undertaker performed his benediction. I could see and hear everything. I might not have been there in flesh, but I was there in spirit.

While I had been a menace the majority of my life, I did achieve one thing - I graduated from high school. I don't know how because I never finished the final exam. To this day I don't know how I managed to pull that off. Maybe there was a mistake when my name was printed with the senior graduating class or maybe it was a cruel prank. I don't know how it happened, but one thing was for certain, I wasn't about to start asking questions. I just put on my cap and gown and waited to hear the principal call my name.

As I sat with my fellow classmates, I reminisced. I reminisced about elementary school and how I had been a straight A student and received numerous awards upon graduating from the sixth grade.

I reminisced of the days when asked "What do you want to be when you grow up?" I would proudly answer, "A doctor or a lawyer."

I reminisced of that fateful day, when I foolishly decided to hook school and thus, naively became a woman. I reminisced of how my life had been a spiraling soap opera, played out for the world to see.

In the midst of my recollection, I heard my name called. I could hardly wait to get up on the stage and walk away with what I felt was rightfully mine. When the principal handed me my diploma, I felt a tremendous sense of reprieve. Finally, after all that I had been through, I did it. I was so proud.

While the other students were signing autographs and exchanging phone numbers, I was rushing out the front door with my family and friends. I didn't want to say goodbye to anyone. I just wanted to get away from there before the principal realized she had possibly made a mistake.

Now that I was out of high school I had to figure out what I wanted to do with the rest of my life. I didn't have the slightest clue. I had thought about going to college, but I didn't want to leave Hasannah for someone else to raise. For a while, I didn't do anything. I worked several dead-end jobs until I ran into Andrew.

Andrew and I met when I was still a student at Cambridge. He was a counselor from Financing Futures, a non-profit organization that worked with students in the D.C. area. I had signed up for an S.A.T. prep class that was being offered in-part by Financing Futures.

One day I went to Cambridge to talk to one of the school counselors and I saw Andrew in the lobby. He asked me what I had been up to and I told him that I was trying to decide whether I wanted to work or go to college.

He told me that he had some information on college grants and awards and he also knew of someone that was hiring. It was Financing Futures. They were looking for a receptionist. I gave Andrew a copy of my resume and he promised to give it to the president of the company.

The next day I received a call from the president of Financing Futures. He said that Andrew had spoken very highly of me and asked if I could come in for an interview. I was there in less than two hours. He was so impressed with me that he asked if I could start working right away. I started the following day.

That was my first experience in the working world. I didn't know much about computers, but I had taken a class or two. Each day I would practice using the computer. After becoming familiar with the keyboard, I started to read the instruction manuals. Before long, I was proficient with several different computer software packages.

In no time, I went from receptionist to office manager. I was given my own office and my first set of business cards. The only problem was that they just increased my title and responsibilities, not my pay. I was still making $8.50 per hour. Whenever I would ask for a raise they would tell me that it wasn't in the budget.

At first it didn't bother me. Even though I wasn't making the money I felt as though I should have been making, I was gaining valuable experience. After all, I was fresh out of high school.

The pay wasn't good, but I had good benefits like health insurance for Hasannah and me. Besides, I was still with Ronnie and living at home with my mother. Although I had pretty much quit boosting, I would take a chance on a cute outfit and a pair of shoes every now and again.

One day Jamillah and I were en route to the mall. Before getting on the freeway, we stopped at a store to get something to eat. When Jamillah pulled into the parking space, she waved at this guy. "Damn, who's that? He's kind of cute," I said.

"That's Randall. We went to school together."

"Really? I've never seen him before. Does he hang around here."

"He used to hang around here a long time ago, but I haven't seen him in a while. That nigga is caked up."

That was all Jamillah needed to say.

Broke as shit and on the prowl for another sugar-daddy, I told Jamillah, "Tell him to come over here when he comes out of the store. I want to talk to him."

When Randall came out of the store Jamillah called him over to the car just as I had told her.

"Hey Randall, what's up with you?" I asked.

"Nothing much. What's up with you?"

"You," I replied seductively.

"Me?" He tried to sound innocent.

"Yes, you."

"Well, in that case, do you have a number where I can reach you?"

"Yeah, but you have to call me at work. My boyfriend is at my house most of the time."

"Oh really? So you have a boyfriend?"

"Yeah, I have a boyfriend. Do you have a girlfriend?"

"Something like that."

We exchanged phone numbers, then Jamillah and I left for the mall.

Later that day, when I got home, I wanted to talk to Randall, but I didn't want to call him first. It was Friday night and if I didn't call him, I would've had to wait for him to call me at work on the following Monday. The suspense was killing me, so after a few hours of contemplating, I gave in and called him.

The first time we talked, we were on the phone for hours. He asked if he could come and see me. Later that night he picked me up. We didn't go anywhere in particular, we just drove around and talked. He seemed so pleasant. We both had someone else, so that made it easier. I didn't have to worry about him trippin' and he didn't have to worry about me. We would be good friends and nothing more.

As the weeks went by, Randall and I grew closer. We would talk everyday and see each other several times a week. He was still with his girlfriend and I was still with Ronnie.

Ronnie knew I was seeing someone else, but as usual, he ignored the signs. I was becoming extremely irritated by Ronnie and was avoiding him whenever possible.

One day I had went on a date with Randall. He was pulling up in front of my house when I noticed Ronnie sitting on the porch. I told Randall not to let me out right there because Ronnie would see me getting out of his car, so Randall drove down the street and let me out in front of my aunt's house. I walked back up the street and sat on the porch with Ronnie.

"Where have you been?" Ronnie asked

"I was down the street at my aunt's house."

"Stop lying, Kerri. I was sitting right here on the porch. I just saw you in the car with another nigga, and I know you saw me!" He was pissed.

I played stupid. "I don't know what you're talking about."

"So what are you saying? Am I hallucinating now?"

"Go' 'head with that shit, Ronnie. Don't nobody feel like arguing with you." I tried to divert the attention away from me.

"Whatever, Kerri. I saw y'all. He pulled up in the front of the house first, then when he saw me on the porch, he took off."

"Whatever, Ronnie. I don't know who it was that you saw, but it wasn't me!"

I didn't know what to do. I was sick of Ronnie and tired of denying it so I just said, "Okay, Ronnie. You caught me. I've been cheating on you."

He looked so disappointed. He turned to me and said, "You aint shit," and walked away.

Later that day Ronnie called. He was hurting and wanted to know why I felt the need to cheat on him. I told him that I had tried to leave him many times and that each time I tried he would make me feel bad for not wanting to be with him. I tried to explain to him that my cheating on him was intentional. That I was trying to please us both.

I knew that Ronnie wanted to be with me, but I wanted to be with Randall. Since Ronnie wouldn't allow me to leave him, my cheating on him was the only thing I could think of to make him leave me. He didn't like what I told him, but he understood. He went on with his life and I didn't hear from him again until years later.

When I dumped Ronnie, Randall was content. We had only been dating for a few months and already we were both developing feelings for each other.

I was approached by other guys, but I wasn't
interested in them. Randall had my full attention, despite his
continued relationship with his girlfriend.

After a few months I told Randall that I couldn't
stand to be his mistress any longer. If he wanted to continue
to see me, he would have to leave his girlfriend.

At first Randall had no intentions on leaving her. He
wanted to have his cake and eat it too. I was so tired of
jumping from one relationship to the next that I just stayed
with him. He assured me that he would eventually leave her,
but it just wasn't the right time.

By now it was December. Randall and I would see
each other practically everyday. Each night he would stay at
my house and leave about 5:00 in the morning, just in time
to sneak in the house before his girlfriend woke up.

Ever so often, I'd get upset with the thought of him
being with her. I was sick of sharing him and wanted him to
myself. One of the reasons that I put up with him having a
girlfriend was that he was taking care of Hasannah and me.

I was still working for Financing Futures and
Hasannah had started attending a new daycare center. The
center was a short bus ride away from my house.

When Randall realized that I had to catch the bus to
get around, he started taking me everywhere I needed to go.
He had several luxury cars and would either take me where I
needed to go or let me drive one of his cars.

Like myself, Randall was very materialistic. He only
drove the best cars and wore the best clothes. He was
attempting to make the transition from illegal money to
legitimate income. He had just purchased a beauty and

barber shop and was well known in the D.C. area as an up
and coming rap artist and producer.

I loved being with Randall. He was so charismatic.
Though I thoroughly enjoyed his company, it was becoming
apparent that he had a drinking problem.

At first I thought he just drank occasionally. Then I
started to notice that he was drinking everyday, and often
several times a day. Just like most alcoholics, he didn't
think he had a problem. When I would tell him that he was
an alcoholic and needed help he would become furious. He
would say, "You trippin'...I aint no goddam alcoholic!"

He would come over to my house late at night and
drunk as hell. Most times, he would be so drunk that I
couldn't believe he had actually made it to my house all in
one piece. He would down a gallon of liquor in less than an
hour. Randall consumed enough alcohol to satisfy ten
people. And, like most alcoholics, he didn't realize what it
was doing to his body nor his mind.

One night Randall had come over to my house pissy
drunk. When I opened the door, he staggered into the living
room and stumbled on the sofa.

"Randall, what is your problem? You need to get
some help!" I said as I shook his arm and told him to get up.

He was so smashed that he just looked up at me,
cracked a crooked smile, and said, "Pass me the Remy."

I sat down on the couch and thought to myself *I've
got to get him some help.*

Randall was so intoxicated that I didn't want him to
drive home, so I told him to lie down on the sofa and I lay
down beside him.

As I was sleeping, I heard some noise coming from
the kitchen. At first I thought I was dreaming, but then I

heard a loud hissing sound. I woke up and went into the kitchen. "What the fuck are you doing?" I screamed at Randall.

"I'm okay, I'm just using the bathroom," he said. He was so inebriated that he could hardly get the words out. There he was right before me, holding the oven door down with one hand and his dick in the other. I couldn't believe what I was seeing - he was pissing in the oven.

"What are you . . . crazy? This is not the bathroom, you idiot! You're pissing in my goddamn oven!" I yelled.

He just looked at me, shook his dick dry, cracked another crooked smile and went back to the sofa. I was revolted.

The next morning I told him what had happened, but he didn't believe me. He couldn't believe that he would do such a thing. Neither could I. If I hadn't seen it with my very own eyes, I wouldn't have believed it either.

After being with Randall for several months, I started to notice other things about him that I didn't like. When I first met him, he seemed like the perfect gentleman. But as time went on I started to see his true colors.

It seemed as if Randall was mad at the world. He had been dealt every bad card in the deck. Like mine, his life had been a series of ups and downs.

As a result of his upbringing, Randall detested his parents. His mother and father were married, but they separated after years of abuse. They never legally divorced and his father went on to be with several different women and created quite a few children. Randall resented that.

When his parents separated, Randall's mother started abusing drugs. According to Randall, she wasn't always an addict. His father, a chronic alcoholic and drug abuser, had turned her on to drugs, and after their separation she began abusing drugs heavily. Randall resented that too.

He didn't know what it was like to have a mother nor a father. They hadn't been there for him. When he was born, his mother left him at the hospital and the nurse had to discharge him to the custody of his grandmother. Though his mom and dad would drop in occasionally, he was raised by his grandparents.

Growing up with his grandparents wasn't effortless. Not only had Randall's parents left him for his grandparents to raise, others in his family left their kids for her to raise too. He grew up in a tiny one bedroom apartment accompanied by several relatives and family friends. He didn't know what it was like to have his own clothes nor his own room. In fact, he didn't have his "own" anything. Everything he had was shared and handed down.

Ordinarily, when people grow up poor and come from broken homes, they pledge allegiance to themselves and the ones they love. They promise not to become mirrors of their own childhoods.

If their father beat their mother, they attest never to lay a hand on their spouse, or if they were constantly short on necessities as children, their refrigerators and closets would be full to capacity as adults. Often, in the course of striving so hard to make good all the bad that had been done to them, they instinctively neglect their mission and consequently duplicate what they experienced as children.

Contrary to his longing to become nothing like his parents, Randall took on several undesirable traits of his mother and grew up to become an avid abuser like his father.

CHAPTER NINE

A wise woman once said, "When you see crazy coming, cross the street." I saw crazy coming all right, however, instead of crossing the street in the opposite direction, I ran smack dead in his path. Before long, I was knee deep in hopeless misery, trapped in his agonizing web of mischief and mayhem.

For Randall, mischief and mayhem was an understatement. Crazy doesn't even begin to describe our relationship. From the very beginning I knew he had issues. All the signs were there, I just chose to ignore them and pretend they didn't exist. I thought that he just needed someone to give him love and understanding. I thought that with a little affection and loyalty, he'd become the person he wanted to be. But the unfruitful seeds of dysfunction had already been planted and it would be a rare occasion that I'd get the chance to see a more deferential side of Randall.

After dating for about six months, he finally left his girlfriend. Three months later we were packing our bags and moving to a small town just outside Atlanta, Georgia.

When I first told my mother that I was leaving she didn't believe me. She knew I was serious when I quit my job and started to pack my things. Soon, everyone knew of my plan to move and I started receiving phone calls from both well-wishers and naysayers.

Most of my family and friends didn't want me to leave. They all thought that it was just a little too soon for me to be moving hundreds of miles away with a man I had only known for nine months. Though no one ever came out and said it, there was a sense of "don't worry, you'll be back" in the air.

When Randall asked me to move to Georgia, I didn't hesitate to say yes. Aside from my family, I didn't have much else going on at that time.

I hadn't even seen pictures of the new house we were moving into. All I knew was that we were in love and he was going to take care of Hasannah and me. I wouldn't have to work or pay bills. I wouldn't have to do much of anything aside from rub his feet and massage his back every once in a while.

When we arrived at the house, I couldn't believe it was actually ours. It was beautiful. I had visited other houses equal in splendor and stature, but never had I actually lived in one. All my life I lived in either low in-come housing or small apartment complexes.

Then, all of sudden, at the innocuous age of 19, I was the head of a 4 bedroom, 3 bathroom house, with 2 fireplaces, a gourmet kitchen and 14' vaulted ceilings. I was astounded.

As we approached the driveway that led to a spacious 2-car garage, I thought *I must be dreaming.* In total disbelief, I asked, "Are you sure this is the house?" He assured me that it was in fact our house as he pressed the remote control button that opened the garage door.

After unloading our things from the car, Randall and I went upstairs. Once again, I was amazed. The inside was more striking than the outside. The house was only one year old. The walls were pristinely white, the kitchen and bathroom appliances were sparkling like new, and the two fireplaces looked as if they had never been used.

The lower level housed a family room, a bedroom and a full bathroom, as well as the laundry facilities. There were three bedrooms on the upper level, including the master bedroom which housed its own private bathroom with a large Jacuzzi-sized soaking tub and separate shower. Hasannah's room was just outside the master bedroom and she too had her own private bathroom. It was a lot for a 19-year-old single mother from Southeast, D.C. to absorb.

Those first few weeks in Georgia were incredible. Everyday was an adventure. We visited all the sites in Atlanta and shopped around for minor additions to our fully furnished house. We planted flowers and herbs for the garden I had always wanted and we bought a dog.

Since Randall would be away in D.C. overseeing his ailing beauty salon/barber shop most of the time, he insisted that we get a watchdog to protect me and Hasannah. I had never owned a dog and didn't know the first thing about taking care of one, but I went along with the plan.

We answered an ad in the paper for a Pitbull puppy
for sale. The owner lived on a nearby farm.
It didn't take me long to choose the puppy I wanted.
There were several puppies for sale, but I decided on the
small black one. He was so cute and cuddly, and his
following me around made me like him even more.

After about a month, we were settled into our new
home. For once in my life I was stable. I had found a good
man who would take care of me and my child. I was living
the American Dream. But as with all dreams, the alarm
clock goes off and eventually you wake up.

CHAPTER TEN

The life I had envisioned to be uncomplicated and blissful turned out to be complexly wretched and miserable.

For starters, I was hundreds of miles away from my family and had yet to meet any new friends. Randall made every effort to fly home every other weekend, but he spent most of his time back in D.C. The only companion I had was Hasannah, and she was only 2 ½-years-old.

Randall didn't want me to work, but I started to get bored so I went out in search of a job. I signed up with several temporary agencies and, in no time, I was working on different assignments each day.

Moving from one assignment to another was good for me. Since I was new to the Atlanta, it gave me a chance to get familiar with the city and its surrounding areas.

Now that I was working, I started to enjoy being there a little more. I was interacting with different people and enjoying the freedom that I had.

Aside from my 2-month stint living with Devin, I had never lived on my own before. Unlike my situation with Devin, I was the head of the household. There was no one to answer to. I made all the decisions, Randall just paid the bills. Besides, technically, he didn't live there. He spent ninety-nine percent of his time in D.C.

Initially, the plan was for me to move to Georgia first, while he stayed in D.C. to run the business he was trying to sell. After he sold the business, he would set up another shop in nearby Atlanta and he'd live in the house with me full time.

As the months passed by, it became evident that the shop would not sell. It was costing more money to keep it open than it would to shut it down so Randall decided to close the shop. He lost the $40,000 he put into the shop, but he was relieved that he didn't have to deal with it anymore. Now that the shop was closed, money was tight. Randall had started to focus his attention on his musical career.

For almost ten years, Randall had been an aspiring rap artist. He recorded an album and had a video featured on the Jukebox, the infamous cable video channel. He received some proceeds from that project and used whatever money he had left to survive for the next few years.

At one point in time he had been a drug dealer, but he had given that up years ago. He was basically your average thug at heart who wanted a better life than what he had been exposed to as a child.

It was now August and I had been living in Georgia

for four months. Randall's visits were becoming more frequent and I had started to get visits from my family and friends.

One day I received a call from Jamie, my second cousin on my mother's side of the family. I hadn't heard from her in years. She had just learned that I had moved and she was curious to know what it was like down south.

Jamie and I began to talk daily. She made plans to visit and a few weeks later she flew down with Randall.

Since we hadn't seen each other for a while, we had a lot of catching up to do. I was so excited. She was one of the first guests I had and I was eager to show-off my new house.

Later that evening, Jamie and I went to the mall while Randall stayed at home with Hasannah. We were having such a good time talking and shopping that we didn't realize the mall was about to close. We left the house around 7:00 that evening. It was a little after 11:00 pm and I had almost forgotten that Randall had cooked dinner and was waiting for me to come home.

Jamie and I talked the whole time back to the house. I told her how I had met Randall. She said that she was glad to see that I was doing well and she even commented on how nice and down-to-earth Randall was. I told her that Randall would probably be a little upset that I didn't call him, but not to mind him if he was fussy because he was just a little overprotective and was not used to me staying out late at night.

I knew that he would be upset, but I had no inkling of the terrifying scene that was about to take place.

When I pulled into the driveway all the lights in the house were out. I was relieved. I thought he must have been asleep. That way, I wouldn't have had to answer any of his silly little questions until the next day. Jamie and I grabbed our bags out of the trunk and headed for the door.

When I opened the door, Randall stood in the foyer and asked, "Where have you been?" I could smell the alcohol on his breath before I stepped inside.

"I was at the mall," I answered.

"Don't lie to me! I'm gonna ask you one more time, where the fuck have you been?" He demanded.

Randall had never spoken to me like that before. Though I was starting to become afraid, I didn't think anything would come of it. I continued to tell him that I was at the mall and had just lost track of time. The more I told him where I had been, the more upset he got until finally, he accused me of being out with another man and forced me into the bedroom.

As soon as we walked into the bedroom he slammed the door. He slammed it so hard that it was almost completely off its hinges.

"Who is he? Who is he?" He demanded.

"Who is who? What are you talking about?"

"You know what I'm talking about!" he yelled while pulling a business card out of my purse.

I shrugged my shoulders. "I don't know! I swear I don't know him! I was walking down the street and he passed me his business card. I didn't even look at it, I just stuffed it in my purse and kept walking."

"What do you think I am? A fool?" Randall was determined to get an answer from me.

"I told you, I don't know him!"

He was two inches from my face when he yelled, "I told you not to lie to me!" Then he balled up his fist and punched me in the mouth. I was stunned.

I tried to punch him back, but the next time he punched me, I was stretched out on the floor. When I came to, he was standing over top of me holding the business card in my face, yelling "Who is he? Who the fuck is he? I knew you were cheating on me! You got so lonely being here all by yourself that you went out and started cheating on me! I knew it! You aint nothing but a ho! I knew I shouldn't have trusted you! I should have left your ass right in Southeast where the fuck I found you! Slutty bitch, I should kill you!" Then he put his hands around my neck and started to choke me.

I was trying to scream, but his hands were wrapped so tightly around my neck that nothing would come out. Then, my ears started to ring and my entire face got numb.

I thought I was dying. I must have passed out because I don't remember what happened after that. When I awoke the next morning, my eye was swollen and my neck felt like someone had tried to chop it off.

Later that day, Randall apologized. He said that he was sorry, but he was worried about me when I didn't call him. That's why he had looked into my purse, to try and find some clue as to where I could be. He said that when he found the business card, he became jealous. He thought that I must have known the man, otherwise why would I have accepted his card. He just kept apologizing for what he had done and promised that it would never happen again.

That night, Jamie, Randall and I all went to a club. We danced and partied all night long. Randall and I looked like the happiest couple. It was as if nothing ever even happened.

Don't ask me why, but I actually believed him when he said he wouldn't hit me anymore. I guess it was because he had never given me any reason to believe that he was a woman beater. Or perhaps it was because he had told me about how his father had abused his mother and how, because of his father, he had vowed to never hit a woman.

That is what was so hard to understand. We had argued before, we even cursed each other out a time or two, but never in my wildest dreams would I have imagined that he would be abusive towards me.

After that first incident we would fight every time he came home. He was still spending most of his time in D.C., but whenever he decided to visit, we'd have knock-down, drag-out fights. The thing that most affronts me is not that he abused me, it's that he did it in front of Hasannah.

When I was Hasannah's age, my mother and Trump used to fight. I would see them brawling and hear them cursing each other out. I can remember how scared I would be and how helpless I felt. I would wonder what my mother had done to deserve such treatment. I also remember feeling that it must have been okay; that men were supposed to beat their women when they stepped out of line. In my 5-year-old mentality, I thought that my mommy was just being punished for misbehaving, just as I had been spanked for doing something I wasn't supposed to do.

How I wish that I had gotten out of that relationship when he first laid his hands on me. It would have saved me years of physical and mental distress.

Each time we'd fight, I'd promise that the next time I

was out of there. But when the next time rolled around, I'd be too afraid to leave.

For a while my family didn't know what was going on. They thought that everything was okay. My mother sensed that something wasn't right and constantly questioned me as to if I was okay, but I was too ashamed to tell anyone and too proud to go back home. I would tell her that everything was fine and that I was just a little homesick.

One weekend I went home to visit everyone. Not much had changed. Everybody was still doing the same things as when I had left. I visited some old friends and hung out with my family. Randall was envious because he said that I wasn't spending any time with him and that I was only concerned with seeing my friends and family. He was right. I didn't want to be bothered with him. I was back in familiar surroundings. For the first time in months I actually felt safe.

Despite the fact that Randall was using me as his personal punching bag, I still loved him. Before the abuse started we discussed the possibility of marriage. I had always dreamed of walking down the aisle in a pretty white dress, pledging my love and dedication to the man of my dreams with my friends and family in the audience cheering me on.

When we arrived back in Georgia that following Tuesday, we decided to get married. Though doubtful, I was hopeful that he would change.

I thought that if we got married, he would treat me differently. I believed that he would have more respect and appreciation for me and life would go as planned.

The elaborate wedding I had always dreamed of turned out to be a low-budget knock-off. There was no pretty white dress, no family and friends cheering me on. I wore a simple pair of jeans and the only audience was Hasannah and a custodian.

As the Justice of the Peace recited the vows, I stood in the foyer of the courthouse and said, "I do."

CHAPTER ELEVEN

When discussing the subject of physical abuse, most people say that if someone were to hit them, they would leave right away and the abuser would never get another chance to hit them again.

I know this to be true because I said the same thing myself. However, I honestly believe that one will never know what they will and will not do until they experience the situation first hand.

Years ago, if someone would have said that I'd grow up to be an abused wife I would have called them a liar. It just wasn't a part of my persona. I had always been an independent, strong willed person. Not the type easily influenced.

Though my mother showered me with love and affection, there was never any order. No discipline to follow, no consequences to take. I wasn't accustomed to taking orders. I pretty much made my own rules. That's

where the trouble with Randall and me began. He needed to
be the dominant figure in our relationship and I refused to
abide. He would demand certain actions and behaviors of
me and I wouldn't conform. When he realized that he
couldn't control me, that's when the abuse stepped in. It was
the only thing that subdued me.

Drinking definitely played a key role in his abuse.
The majority of our fights would commence after he had
consumed large quantities of alcohol. He was not what you
call a social drinker. He drank everyday.
After we married not much changed. He was still
drinking and taking all of his frustrations out on me.
Randall was under an extreme amount of pressure.
Not only had his business gone belly-up, his musical career
wasn't blossoming at the rate at which he had expected. He
spent countless hours in recording studios paying outrageous
fees. He sent innumerable demo tapes to recording agencies.
Though he wasn't getting the response he desired, he never
gave up hope. He was investing all of his time and money
into his music, meanwhile, there was still the small matter of
the mortgage to pay.

Right after we married, I went back to D.C. for a
while. Since the shop was closed, Randall had to start
making money the best way he knew how - dealing drugs.
Randall was making the monthly payments on the house, so
we decided to stay with my mother.
Soon, the abuse I tried so hard to hide from my
family was plain to see. Randall's behavior had worsened.
It started with minor things like him telling me what to wear
and what not to eat.
Asking me not to wear a tight shirt was one thing, but

forbidding me to eat certain foods was simply intolerable. I
didn't understand his logic. Though he wouldn't even
consider eating a beef patty or sinking his teeth into a pork
chop because "it's not good for your health," he would drink
enough alcohol to fill a swimming pool and smoke enough
marijuana to pack a chimney. Now you tell me, how much
sense did that make?

Then, it progressed to him telling me what I could
and could not look at. For instance, if we were in a mall or
someplace similar, he would accuse me of staring at other
men. I tried to explain to him that I wasn't staring at anyone
in particular and that I was only surveying my surroundings.

He insisted that when I was with him I should not
worry about my surroundings. I should be proud to be in his
presence and that my looking at other men made him feel
inferior. Randall was such a control freak that he couldn't
bear the fact that I had a mind of my own. His meager
attempts to not allow me to be the person that I was
frustrated me.

In the beginning of the abuse he would simply beat
the crap out of me and I would do whatever it took to make
him happy. After a while I grew tired of being abused. If
we were having an argument, instead of waiting for him to
punch me, I began to punch him first.

When I started to fight back, that made him even
more furious. Here I was 120 pounds and I had the nerve to
assault him.

He stood only 5'10" tall, but he was no small man.
Before I met Randall, he had been slightly overweight, but
by the time we hooked up he had slimmed down
considerably. In fact, he had gone from forty inches to a size
thirty- four, with bulging biceps and a washboard waist. He

exercised daily and had a body that just wouldn't quit. But soon, the liquor started to take a toll on his frame.

My mom had asked us to pay her $100 a month for rent. Since I wasn't making much money working odd jobs, Randall agreed to pay.

He rarely paid her on time, but she never complained. He would have the money put away, but for whatever reason, he refused to pay. Eventually, he and my mom started to have verbal disagreements and before long she asked us to leave.

By now it was the beginning of February and I was 20-years-old. I had just been hired as an administrative assistant for an upscale hotel chain. We moved into an apartment in nearby Landover, Maryland.

Randall's feuding with my mom started to take its toll on me. I tried to remain neutral, but he practically forbade me to see her and whenever I talked to my mother, she tried her best to convince me to leave him.

That was a tough situation to deal with. I loved them both and didn't want to lose either of them. Randall thought that since he was my husband, I should've been on his side. My mother felt like no man should come between a mother and daughter, so she thought I should have sided with her. It was an impossible predicament. I didn't know how to handle it. On one end, you have the man you have vowed to be with for eternity and on the other end, you have the woman who gave you life. They were constantly bickering back and forth and I was the rope in their bitter tug of war.

My grandmother once told me, "Never trust a man who doesn't respect his mother."

I started to realize that not only did Randall have no

respect for his own mother, he had no respect for mine. In fact, he had no respect for women period.

I believe he loved his mother, but he hated the life she created for him. She never spent any time with him and he never got a chance to know who she really was.

As a child, the other women in his life tried to make up for the damage his mother had done. Despite their efforts, it wasn't enough. No amount of love from his aunts and grandmother could heal his broken adolescent heart. Regardless of how hard his family tried to repair his erratic spirit, Randall craved for attention and yearned for the love of his parents.

I had discovered that I was pregnant. We were living in a one-bedroom apartment and already it was crowded.

When I learned I was expecting another child, it eased some of my worry. I thought for sure that Randall would calm down at least for the next nine months. I thought that no man in his right mind would beat his pregnant wife. I just knew that my pregnancy would force him to change, but I was wrong. Randall didn't calm down one bit. He actually got worse.

I used to dread coming home from work. Each day, Randall would have something to argue about. It could have been something as minuscule as running out of toilet paper. He would make the biggest deal out of everything. He didn't care how it made me feel. His life was going down hill and he was determined to take me with him.

One day, after work, I went to the grocery store. When I came home Randall was in the bedroom watching television. I must have had about eight bags of groceries, and he didn't lift one finger to help me. By this time, I was about five months pregnant.

I was in the kitchen putting the food away when Randall walked in. I could tell he had been drinking so I braced myself for whatever half-witted act he was about to commit.

For a minute he didn't say or do anything, he just stood in the doorway and watched me. Then he saw me take some orange juice out of a bag.

"What kind of juice is that?" he asked.

I thought to myself *Please, Randall, not today.*

Before I could even produce an answer he snatched the orange juice out of my hand and started to perform, "What is this shit? You know I don't drink this kind of orange juice!" Then he went utterly out of control.

He took the jug of juice and poured it out on the floor. Then he threw an entire carton of eggs at the wall, one by one. He poured milk and flour on top of the juice on the floor and proceeded to call me all sorts of names in the process.

I didn't say a word. I just stood there watching him, wondering why he was behaving like a nincompoop.

Then he looked at me and said, "The next time you bring some cheap ass juice in this house, your ass will be the one on the floor! Now get in here and clean this shit up!"

I couldn't believe him. After he had lost his mind and destroyed the kitchen, he had the nerve to tell me to clean it up. I was disgusted. However, I knew that if I didn't clean it up I would have had to fight him. So, with my aching feet and swollen belly, I grabbed the mop and broom and started cleaning.

As I sit here reminiscing, remembering the explicit

horror I once experienced, I can't believe I actually put up with that kind of treatment.

It has been said that women who are abused are in an affliction. It is a disease called Battered Women's Syndrome. I am truly one who believes that society has too many labels, too many titles and too many syndromes.

Why does a woman stay with a man who beats her? Why doesn't she leave her abuser? Why do women believe their abusers when they promise to never hit them again? These are questions for which I have no answer. I can't speak for all women, but I can surely speak for myself.

For starters, I was only 19-years-old when the abuse started. Age alone gives some insight as to why I accepted it. Secondly, I was in love and, as we all know, love is blind. Lastly, I thought I could change him. Those were nine of the worst months of my life. Randall and I fought daily and the abuse had started to wear me down.

One day Randall had been drinking and was looking for something to argue about. I knew he was drunk so I tried my best to stay out of his way. I was in the bedroom combing Hasannah's hair when he walked in. He picked an argument with me and before I knew it, we were slugging like two boxers in a ring. I had punched him in the nose so hard that it started to bleed. When he saw the blood streaming down his face he went ballistic. He grabbed his gun from under the mattress and pointed it at me. I was screaming and telling him to put the gun away. Then, he grabbed me by the hair and put the gun against my pregnant stomach.

"Randall, please . . . please, put the gun away!" I screamed. I was crying and begging him to stop. Hasannah was sitting in the corner crying, covering her big brown eyes with her tiny 3-year-old hands.

He was so upset that I had busted his nose that he threatened to kill me. He held the gun against my back and forced me out the front door. Once we were outside I tried to run, but he ran behind me and grabbed my arm. Then he forced me into the car.

He kept the gun pointed at me while he drove at unbelievable speeds. "I'mma kill you, bitch! You gonna die tonight! You wanna bust my nose and scratch my face up, you gonna die!"

He was speeding down the highway with no apparent destination. I was sitting in the back of the car while Hasannah sat in the front seat. Trying to figure a way to get out of the speeding car without hurting myself, I pleaded with Randall to stop the car.

He was so determined to get back at me for busting his nose that he had no regard for Hasannah nor his unborn child. He turned onto a one-way street and started to slow down. "Get the fuck out!" he yelled as he slammed on the brakes.

Since I was in the back seat it was difficult for me to maneuver. I desperately wanted to get out of the car and as far away from him as possible, but I was hesitant because I knew that he would try to pull off before I was completely out of the car.

I stepped one foot on the ground. "Please, don't pull off before I'm completely out," I begged.

He just kept telling me to get out of the car.

Then, as I placed one foot on the ground with the other foot still in the car, Randall pulled off with Hasannah in the front seat.

I almost fell to the ground, but I managed to catch my

balance. I cradled my abdomen and took off running. As I was running the down the street I saw a car approaching. The driver saw me too, so he pulled over.

There were two girls and two guys in the car. The driver rolled down his window and asked if I was okay.

"No! My husband is trying to kill me!" I screamed.

"Where is he now?" The driver was skeptical.

"I don't know, he just drove down the street."

"Come on, I'll take you to the police station."

Just as I was approaching the car, Randall came speeding around the corner driving up the one-way street in the wrong direction. He jumped out of his car, "Come here Kerri," he said with his gun in his hand.

When the driver of the other car saw Randall's gun, he took off speeding down the street.

I had almost gotten away, but Randall was determined to get even. He walked up to me, picked me up and threw me in the back seat.

As he drove through the quiet residential streets, I punched and kicked the back of his seat. I was screaming for him to let me out of the car and he pulled over.

He jumped out of the driver's seat and opened the back door. "Okay, bitch. You wanna fight, let's fight!" he said as he reached in the backseat and choked me. I was punching, kicking and biting, doing everything I could think of to get him off of me.

"I'mma kill you, bitch!" he said as he wrapped his manly hands around my neck. Then, with his butterscotch Timberland boots, he tried to stomp me, but I grabbed a pencil I saw on the floor and stabbed him in the leg.

"Ouch! You fucking bitch! I'mma kill your ass!"

We fought for what seemed like hours. I was so exhausted that I just gave up. Randall was just as tired as I was so he got back in the driver's seat and sped away. This time, he was headed for the freeway.

It was the middle of summer and the windows were rolled up and there was no air circulating. I was a chronic asthmatic so I was in the back seat gasping for my breath. When he saw me struggling to breathe, he turned the heat on full blast, "One way or another, your ass is gonna die tonight!" he promised.

I knew that if he really wanted me to die he would have killed me when he had the chance. I knew that he was just talking shit and blowing off steam in his own neurotic way. I also knew that if I didn't get some air soon I would die for real so I stopped talking, held my breath and pretended to be dead.

When he didn't hear me breathing anymore he panicked. He thought he had really killed me. By this time we were in the parking lot of our apartment complex. He pulled into a parking space and opened the door.

He got in the back seat and started to cry. "Oh, Kerri. I'm so sorry, baby. Please, don't die on me, I'm sorry." He shook me and told me to wake up. I wanted to teach him a lesson so I lay there with my eyes closed pretending to be unconscious.

Randall cried uncontrollably and asked God to forgive him. At that point, I felt that he had learned his lesson and I opened my eyes.

When he saw that I was still alive he was relieved.

He held me in his arms and gave me a big hug. He apologized for what he had done and asked me to forgive him. He took Hasannah out of the front seat and apologized to her and then he placed his lips on my stomach and kissed his unborn child. After hours of horrific torture, his high had gone down and he was completely sober.

After that incident Randall calmed down considerably. Months passed and we hadn't fought one time. I was growing accustomed to the new Randall and hopeful that he was there to stay. I soon discovered that the old Randall was simply on hiatus and the new Randall had no plans to stick around.

CHAPTER TWELVE

Ninth months into my pregnancy, America was about to witness the largest gathering of black men ever recorded in history. It was the day of the highly anticipated Million Man March. The media held it as one of the largest gatherings of any kind to embrace U.S. soil. Black men from everywhere in the country came to D.C. to unite as one.

It was beautiful. Never before had so many Black men united with such optimism to discuss pertinent political issues as well as to celebrate the beauty and mysticism of the existence of our people. I was inspired.

As Randall prepared to attend the Million Man March, I felt a sense of pride. My husband, the once abusive, drug dealing peril, was participating in something positive. I gave him a big hug and kiss as he walked out the door.

As I watched the unprecedented event on television, I couldn't help but be excited. I was amazed that such an event was actually taking place and even more amazed that Randall was a part of it.

Later that evening, Randall returned. After the March, he had accompanied some of his friends out for drinks. As soon as he walked in the door he was complaining about the house not being clean. I knew that he was just looking for something to argue about so I went in the bedroom and closed the door. When he realized I wasn't listening to him he tried to come in the bedroom, but I had locked the door and he couldn't get in.
"Open this goddamn door!" he yelled.
"Not until you go somewhere and calm down."
Randall was annoyed. He gave one last warning.
"You'd better open this door before I knock it down!"
As I sat on the bed reading a book, he banged on the door. He kept banging and I kept reading, pretending that he wasn't there. Then, I heard a loud crash. He had kicked the door down.
"I told you to open the door! Your ass is gonna get it now!"
I didn't wait for him to punch me, I took the book I was reading and threw it at him. After three months of absolutely no physical assault, we were at it again. So much for atonement and honoring the black woman.

Though that was the sentiment the Minister Louis Farrakahn preached at the Million Man March, it would take more than one day of male bonding to change Randall.
In spite of my hopes and prayers, the new Randall

had disappeared and the old Randall was back in town.

Though I was abused throughout that pregnancy, I gave birth to a healthy baby girl. We named her Randa. Now there were four of us living in that tiny one-bedroom apartment.

We still had the house in Georgia and had planned to go back there sooner or later. Since I was working for a national hotel chain, I planned to put in for a transfer to one of the hotels it operated in Georgia.

Now that Randa was here we were really struggling. Randall was still paying the majority of the bills, with the exception of the rent for the apartment. I was making about twenty thousand dollars a year, so the five hundred dollar monthly rent on the apartment was handled by me.

At one time, we were so desperate for money that Randall had to sell his truck. For a while, we didn't have an automobile and public transportation was our only means to get around.

One morning while standing at the bus stop, I ran into Lisa, the girl I befriended at Cambridge High School. Years ago, we became good friends after leaving school and hanging out during school hours.

She lived only a few blocks away and we were waiting for the same bus.

We were so happy to see each other. I hadn't seen her since high school. We exchanged phone numbers and began talking everyday.

Lisa and I had never been very close. After I graduated we lost contact. But as I have always suspected, God brings certain people into your life for specific reasons.

At the time, I didn't know what her purpose in my life was nor why we had crossed each other's paths. I was just glad to see her. But in the months to come, it would become clear why God had arranged a renewal of our acquaintance.

Soon, we would discover that we had a lot in common. As I had just given birth to a new baby, she was only months away from experiencing the joys of motherhood. As I had fallen in love with a controlling, abusive tyrant, she was dating his evil twin. And as I was in constant disagreement with my mother, she too was plagued by her mother's interference.

Over the next few years, Lisa and I would become inseparable. We were both in abusive relationships so we understood each other's pain. Whenever I would have an argument with Randall, I would run to Lisa for comfort and whenever she had a disagreement with Leo, I'd be the first to know about it.

We would talk about how much Randall and Leo had in common, how they treated us like shit and possessed similar personalities.

Lisa's mother hated Leo just as much as my mother despised Randall. After her daughter was born, she moved out into her first apartment.

Like me, you couldn't tell Lisa shit. She was brought up a lot like me. In other words, she was fast. Infatuated with the lavish lifestyle afforded to drug dealers and their women, Lisa worshiped Leo. He spent all of his money on her and she loved every minute of it.

Aside from perversion, Leo was cunning. Like Randall, he knew just what to say and do to make Lisa weak in the knees. He would spend the dough and sex her all night, pay her bills and even bought her a car.

Though he was physically and verbally abusive, he
showered her with gifts. He would make up for the hurt
feelings and black eyes with good sex and shopping sprees.
Lisa's desperate quest for a thug's love and the material
rewards that come with it blinded her to Leo's true being.
Their relationship was traveling at the speed of light and
going nowhere fast.

Randall and I continued to fight like cats and dogs.
Nonetheless, we were still together. Finally, a position had
opened at one of the Georgia properties. Desperate to get
away from Randall, I rushed to submit my application.

After reviewing my resume and the impressive letter
of recommendation forwarded by my supervisor, I was asked
to do a phone interview. The hotel's Director of Sales was
so impressed with my qualifications and enthusiasm that I
was flown down to Georgia to be interviewed in person.

When I came back to D.C. I knew I had the job. It
hadn't been officially offered to me yet, I just knew it. The
next day I received a phone call from the Director of Sales of
the Georgia property. Just as I had expected, the job was
mine.

I didn't tell anyone of my plan to move back down
south. I just made silent arrangements and planned to start
working at the well-known hotel two weeks later.

Before my departure I wanted to go out and celebrate
with Lisa. She and I had become extremely close and I was
going to miss her terribly.

Lisa was happy that I had gotten the job I wanted, but
she was sad to see me go. Without me around, whom would
she call when Leo pissed her off? Whose shoulder would

she cry on when Leo mistook her for a doormat? And who would help her pull herself together after she had just gotten the taste buds slapped out of her mouth?

Despite Leo's wishes, a few nights before I left town, Lisa and I went out to a club. Lisa's father was at her house and agreed to babysit Hasannah and Randa while we went out to celebrate. So with our short shorts and tight shirts, we set out to find the perfect club to dance the night away.

We left the club about 4:00 in the morning. Lisa was terrified that Leo would be waiting for her at the front entrance of her apartment so we decided to park in the rear of the building.

Before exiting the car, we looked around, carefully canvassing the area for Lisa's possessive mate. Since there was no sign of Leo, we jumped out and ran in the building. As soon as we got inside Lisa checked her Caller I.D. to see if he had called. He did, a grand total of thirteen times.

She decided to wait until morning to return Leo's calls, but he beat her to it. He called at 8:00 that morning.

I was still asleep when I heard Lisa on the telephone arguing with Leo. The kids were asleep and so was Lisa's father. Lisa was cursing Leo out so bad and talking so loud that she woke up everyone in the house.

I asked her if everything was okay and she said that she just had to make him a little jealous. She hardly ever went out and he was having a hard time dealing with her assertiveness.

Then as Lisa and I lay on the bed talking, Leo barged in the bedroom door. Hasannah and Randa were on the bed as well, while Lisa's daughter swung happily in her baby swing.

Leo picked Lisa's small body off the bed and yelled, "What the fuck you showing off for?"

She tried to free herself from Leo's grip. "Get your fuckin' hands off of me!" she screamed.

Then, Leo hauled off and slapped her in the face. She tried to hit him back, but he threw her in the corner and released an arsenal of punches.

I was frantically trying to get the kids into another room when Lisa's father walked in. He tried to stop Leo from beating Lisa, but Leo pulled a gun from his waste and threatened, "Step the fuck back or I'll kill 'ery body up in this motherfucker!"

We were begging Leo to stop hitting Lisa and trying to convince him to put the gun away, but he wouldn't listen. He pushed us out the bedroom and slammed the door.

I sat in the living room trying to figure out a way to help Lisa. I felt so helpless hearing Leo pound his enormous fists upon Lisa's frail body. I wanted to help her, but there was nothing I could do because Leo had a gun.

Lisa was crying and screaming for help. The kids were crying so I tried my best to calm them down. I ran out into the hall and knocked on every door in sight. No one answered. Some even told me to get away from their door.

I was crying and begging them to let me in; telling them that Leo was beating Lisa and that there were kids in the house. No one cared. I went back into Lisa's apartment and waited in the living room. Then, all of a sudden, it got quiet. Lisa stopped crying and I didn't hear anymore fighting. I thought the awful nightmare was over when suddenly Leo came running out of the bedroom with the gun in his hand. I grabbed the kids and sat on the couch.

He walked over to me and put the gun up to my head. "You freak ass bitch, I should kill you! It's your fault that she went out to a club! Don't be coming up her influencing my girl to go out to no goddamn club shaking her ass like some little slut!"

I just sat there and looked at him like the neurotic asshole that he was. Then he took the gun and put it up to Hasannah's temple. "Yeah, yeah, say something! I'll blow her little fuckin' brains out! Say something! I dare you!"

He held the gun steady against Hasannah's head. Tears ran down her face as she screamed, "Mommmiiieee! Please don't let him kill me!"

At that point, I completely lost it. I didn't give a fuck who he thought he was or what he had in his hand. I was not going to sit back and watch him torment my baby so I jumped up and grabbed the handle of the gun.

"Let the gun go, bitch!"

"No motherfucker, you let it go!" I gripped that gun with all my might.

"You better let it go before I pull the trigger!" he warned.

It didn't take me long to make my next move. I bit his wrist and kicked him in the balls as hard as I could.

"Ow! You fuckin' bitch, I'mma kill your ass!"

He grabbed his crouch in pain and I snatched the gun from his hands.

"Yeah, motherfucker! Talk shit now!" I felt like superwoman.

"Bitch, fuck you!" he yelled.

I cocked a bullet into the chamber and pointed the gun directly at him. "Yeah, motherfucker! You ain't so bad now! Say something! I dare you!" Just as he did to

Hasannah, I centered the barrel between his eyebrows. "Go 'head motherfucker, try me! I dare you! I'll blow your fuckin' brains out!"

You could have heard a pin drop.

Though I was accustomed to physical abuse, no one had ever threatened the lives of my children.

I held the gun steady, pointing it at Leo's head like a target. I then grabbed the kids and dashed over to the front door. Before I walked out I yelled for Lisa. "Lisa, it's safe now. Come on, let's get out of here."

"You better not come out here, Lisa!" Leo yelled.

Then Lisa's father came out into the living room. He looked at me with the gun in my hand and then at Leo. He looked back to me again and said, "Damn, Kerri. How did you get the gun?"

I didn't answer, I just motioned for him to follow me.

Just as we were about to walk out the door Lisa's father said, "Hold on a second. I forgot something." He walked over to Leo and punched him in the mouth.

Leo jumped up and was about to punch him back when I warned, "If you even think about hitting him, I'll shoot you dead." He rolled his eyes and sat back down.

Lisa was still in her bedroom afraid to come out. Once again I yelled for her to come with me and Leo told her to stay put.

I walked into the hall and began knocking on doors again. Luckily, Lisa's next door neighbor heard what was going on and invited me in. I was so terrified that I was shaking all over. She offered me a glass of water then I called the police.

When the police arrived Lisa answered the door. With a swollen eye and busted lip, she stood right there in my face and called me a liar. She said that she had not been fighting her boyfriend and that she was okay.

Although she was severely bruised to the point that even Ray Charles could see, she wasn't willing to admit it. Since she wouldn't implicate Leo as a suspect the police had nothing to go on. They just said okay and went on about their business to protect and serve.

I was disappointed, but I definitely understood. In her abused, brainwashed mind, that was the last time. Like so many last times before that one, she promised herself that she would leave him. But just as with every other last time, it wasn't.

Despite Lisa's desire to leave Leo, she loved him. And he knew it. He knew that no matter what he did to her, Lisa wasn't going anywhere. So after that supposedly last time, there would be another last time...then another...and another.

Though I was disturbed with the events that took place at Lisa's apartment that Saturday morning, I never said a word about it to Randall.

Leo didn't know it, but Randall was just as crazy, if not crazier, than he was. If I would have told Randall that Leo had cursed me out in front of the kids, Randall would have been two seconds off Leo's behind. And if Randall would have known that Leo had threatened to kill me and even had the nerve to put a gun up to Hasannah's head, Leo's mother would've been singing sad songs, searching for a suit and paying for a casket.

The day before I left town Lisa called me. She was afraid for her life and wanted to know if she could move to Georgia with me. Though I sympathized with her, I didn't think it was a good idea. For starters, Randall still didn't know about what had happened and I planned on keeping it that way. Besides, Randall and I fought too, so she would have been going from the frying pan into the fire.

So after a terrifying week of events, I packed my things and moved back to our house in Georgia.

Randall wouldn't be able to join me for several months. That was the main reason why I wanted to go back to Georgia because it would allow me to get away from Randall and have some time alone to get my thoughts together. Since school was out, Randall's teenage cousin Malcolm agreed to stay with me for the summer and babysit the girls while I worked.

I was enjoying my new job and the friends I had acquired. Malcolm was good with the kids and provided me with company as well. Everything was going fine until the weekend Randall came home to visit.

My cousin Kimmie rode down with Randall. We had planned a fun-filled weekend, but Randall decided on something more sinister.

It was Friday evening and I had just come in from work. Malcolm, Kimmie and Randall were playing cards and having a good time. I was pleased to see that Randall was not drinking and actually trying to behave himself. We all sat around and talked for a while.

Then, Randall decided that he had remained sober for long enough. When I saw him go into the kitchen I knew he was about to start boozing. Since things were going well I asked him to try and refrain from drinking.

Randall didn't pay me any mind. He went into the cabinet where he kept his liquor and poured a glass. He quickly guzzled the first glass down and started on a second. Before long, he had nearly finished a 3-liter bottle of liquor all to himself. Soon, the liquor started to settle and everyone could tell that he was drunk.

He began talking in circles. Then he began talking so loud, that he could have awaken the dead. He started to make such a spectacle of himself that I practically forced him to go and lay down.

After begging and pleading with him, he gave in and went into the bedroom to take a nap, but that only lasted a few minutes. In no time he was back out in the living room reaping havoc on everyone in the household. Malcolm and Kimmie were becoming annoyed by Randall's antics so they left the room and went downstairs.

As soon as they were out of the room, Randall started to verbally attack me. Once again, he accused me of cheating. I was so accustomed to his drunken charades that I just sat there and ignored him. The more I overlooked his insipid behavior, the more insidious he became.

At one point, he was so disturbed with my apparent equanimity that he practically begged me to argue with him. I'd had about as much of his absurdity as I could stand so I just got up and walked away.

As I was leaving the bedroom I heard him running behind me. As I turned around he lunged forward and tried to punch me, but he was so drunk that he stumbled to the floor. I jumped over him and ran into the kitchen.

I knew that he would try to fight me so I grabbed a knife. He must have heard me fumbling through the silverware because when he came out of the bedroom it was as if he was a soldier in World War II.

Clutching his Tech Nine machine gun with the force

of a dead man's grip, and moving through the house with
militant precision, Randall jumped from behind corners and
moved like clockwork. In a steady, determined tone, he
chanted "Kerri? Come out, come out wherever you are."

Amazingly enough, seeing his gun didn't scare me.
It was routine for him to brandish a gun whenever we fought.
But hearing him chant that ridiculous mantra and seeing the
look of combat in his eyes made me realize that I was in for
the fight of my life.

As I stood in the kitchen trying to figure a way out,
he walked slowly towards me. Then I gripped my knife and I
said to him, "If you don't leave me alone, I swear to God, I'll
stab your simple ass!"

He kept moving towards me. I figured that if he was
going to shoot me he would have done it by then. I told him,
"Drop the gun and fight me like a man." When he saw me
drop the knife he dropped the gun.

I tried to run downstairs, but he caught me. I must
have made it to about the third step before he pushed me and
I fell down the complete flight of stairs. When I got up, the
first thing I saw was a large vase sitting on the table. I
picked it up and aimed for his head.

He punched me and I punched him back. I managed
to free myself from the brawl and run downstairs to where
Malcolm and Kimmie were.

When they realized we were fighting, they were
scared. Randall came down the stairs and we started fighting
again. Malcolm and Kimmie were too afraid to do anything.
The kids were downstairs with us as Malcolm and Kimmie
tried to keep them calm.

When Randall turned his back I ran outside. I sat on the front steps and started to cry. I could hear them in the house calling me. They were trying to see if I was okay, but I didn't answer. I just sat on the porch and tried to pull myself together.

After a few minutes, Kimmie saw me sitting outside. She was holding 8-month-old Randa in her arms. Randa started crying for me so I took her from Kimmie and started to rock her. As I sat on there crying with Randa in my arms, Randall opened the front door. Before I could move, he kicked me in the back and Randa fell out of my arms onto the ground. Her little lungs howled as Kimmie picked her up and ran back in the house.

Randall and I started fighting again. I managed to free myself and run into the garage.

I proceeded to look for something to hit him with. When I realized he was behind me, I took off running. Randall chased me with a weed wacker yelling, "I'mma kill you, bitch!" I turned around and grabbed his face.

I pulled and scratched until my fingers stung from the cuts. I was scratching and pulling his skin so hard that my hands were covered in blood. The combination of his funky body sweat and the lacerating scratches he received from my finely manicured nails overwhelmed him as he ran into the house screaming, "Help. Help. That bitch is crazy!"

I knew that I had to get away from him. I was so terrified that I planned to kill him if he didn't kill me first. So, in my nightgown and bare feet, I ran to my next door neighbor's house.

I didn't know my neighbor too well. We saw each

other occasionally, but were never formerly introduced. When she came to the door I begged her to let me in. I told her that I needed to use her phone because my husband was beating me. She didn't even hesitate. She opened the door and I went straight to the phone.

Sitting in a chair near the window, talking to the 911 operator, I saw Randall outside looking for me. He was walking around the yard looking behind the trees and bushes, calling my name, asking me to come to him. I just sat in the window crying, waiting for the police to arrive.

When I saw the patrol cars pull up I ran outside. It seemed as if everyone in the cul-de-sac was outside watching. It was the most excitement the residents on my street had ever seen. In a neighborhood that was as quiet as a catholic church during Midnight Mass, there was an uncommon crime scene. Four patrol cars with two police each showed up.

Since the police were there I felt safe. I started telling them what had happened and why I had called them. As I described the tumultuous stage show that had just taken place I noticed that the officers were more concerned with Randall's facial scratches than with my story. I told them that Randall had threatened me with a gun and that he started hitting me first. I told them about his drinking problem and his history of abuse.

Even though I mentioned the fact that Randall had an unregistered gun in the house, they didn't care. They were only interested in finding out what had happened to Randall and why his face was a bloody mangled mess.

I didn't understand why the police weren't listening to me. Randall had beat me so badly that I was in a tremendous amount of pain, despite the fact that I didn't look like it. I kept telling them, "Look at my face, look at what he did to me." The pain was so poignant that I just knew I had a black eye and busted lip. What I didn't realize was that I didn't have any visual scars.

My face ached terribly, but there were no bruises, no knots, not even a lonesome scratch. We had fought like a Don King Main Event, but I didn't look the part. I looked as if nothing had happened to me, but Randall's face was disfigured. He had scratches everywhere.

When the police couldn't find any visual war marks on my body, they were convinced that I was the abuser and locked me up instead. I was outraged.

The officer read me my rights. Randall started arguing with the other police and telling them not to lock me up, to take him instead. When the officer drove away with me in the back of the police cruiser Randall went ballistic.

They arrested Randall too. But he wasn't being arrested for assault and battery as was I, he was being arrested for disorderly conduct. When I got to the police station I saw the other patrol car pull up with Randall sitting in the rear.

Waiting to be fingerprinted, Randall tried to talk to me. I was so insulted by his simulated attempt of reconciliation that I asked to be moved to another holding cell.

Later that night I was released on bail, but Randall was detained for one more day.

I didn't know what I was going to do, but I had to get away from him. Our relationship had always been turbulent, but things had gotten extremely out of hand. So after a year of constant abuse, I had finally come to my senses.

CHAPTER THIRTEEN

I decided to go back home. I didn't give it much thought, I just packed everything I could fit into my car and started my 12-hour journey from the little house of horrors to the security of my Uncle Mack's house in Washington, D.C. Naturally, when I told him I was coming back to D.C. and needed a place to stay, he offered me a room at his house.

I arrived at Mack's house late that night and settled my meager belongings into my new bedroom. I had left practically everything I owned back in Georgia, but I didn't realize it until I started unpacking.

Feeling gutted and dejected, I lay down on my uncle's bed with 3 ½-year-old Hasannah and 8-month-old Randa at my side. As the tears scurried down my worn out face, I asked myself *Why me?*

I was baffled. Once again, I had taken a fall. And the thing I dreaded most had happened; I had proven everyone right. They all said I would be back and here it was, no less than two years later, I was back for good.

Of my many talents, I am most proud of my phenomenal ability to pick up the pieces. I have seen many highs and have endured many lows, but what never ceases to amaze me is my utterly diligent tenacity. No matter how bad things would get, I refused to give up. I couldn't. Surrender was not part of my vocabulary.

Though I cried myself to sleep that first night at Uncle Mack's house, I woke up the next morning with a new attitude. Gone were the feelings of worthless destitution and hopeless depression. I had come to the conclusion that if I was ever going to get out of the rut that I was in I would have to be my own heroine. No one else could rescue me. Not my mother nor my grandmother. Not even Randall. I had to save myself.

For years I'd wondered why my life had been a never-ending crisis. Suddenly I realized that the majority of my wounds were self-inflicted. I was starting to see that, although I loved myself dearly, I was my own worst enemy.
Whenever common sense and good judgment threatened the state of my superficial happiness I would disregard my intuition and satisfy my crave for instant gratification.
"So what if he sells drugs for a living," I would tell myself. "Who cares if he drinks too much and smokes marijuana," I claimed. Though my ideal mate wouldn't possess these characteristics, at that point in my life, every guy I had ever dated did.

After examining my life more closely I realized that I was attracting those no good men as a result of the negative vibes I was putting out.

In an effort to get back on the right track, I started looking for a job. I had only been back in town for one day and had already contacted several hotels with regards to available employment. After talking to a human resources rep at an upscale hotel in nearby Arlington, Virginia, I got dressed in a borrowed suit and prepared for 20-minute ride to apply for the sales assistant position.

I sat on the subway, en route to my interview, thinking about my plan. At that particular moment I didn't have one, but I knew I had to get one real soon.

The interview went well.

That was the one good thing about me, if I couldn't do anything else, I could always get a job. The interview went so well that they offered me the job on the spot and I started working a few days later.

CHAPTER FOURTEEN

A few weeks past and I was just getting settled into my new job. I hadn't seen Lisa since that Saturday morning when Leo lost his mind so I decided to give her a call.

We decided to hook up and do a repeat of our last night together. We made plans for her to meet me at Mack's house and from there we would go dancing at the Ritz nightclub in downtown D.C.

I was glad to see Lisa. It had been almost two months since we'd seen each other and so much drama had taken place. As Randall and I were going through our ordeal down in Georgia, she and Leo were experiencing problems as well. But for that one night we vowed to forget about our miserable lives and dance our blues away.

We were getting ready to leave Mack's house when Lisa said, "I need to lay down."

"What's wrong, Lisa? Are you okay?" I asked.

"I'm alright, I just have a slight headache."

"Are you sure you wanna go out tonight? We can do this some other time."

"Yes, I'm sure. I need to go out and have some fun. I've been so stressed lately. I just need to take a couple of aspirin."

Lisa took some Tylenol and we left for the club. We were dressed to kill; me in a form fitting dress, with fierce Gucci pumps, and Lisa in pants that were so tight they looked like they were painted on with a magician's wand.

The club was crowded. There were people dancing everywhere and the bar was full of wanna-be pimps and part-time playas. I had gotten my fill of the second hand smoke and foul smelling breath near the bar so we moseyed on to the other side of the club. At least the men on that side of the club didn't all look like rejects from a low-budget 1970's blackploitation film.

We were standing against the wall catching up on each other's lives when all of a sudden "Knock Some Boots" blared from the enormous speakers. We both liked that song so we found our way to the dance floor and danced like nobody's business.

Just as we were ready to sit down and catch our breath, the D.J. switched to Frankie Beverly and Maze's "Before I Let Go" so you know we didn't go nowhere. We partied like we had just hit the lottery.

After dancing to a few more jams, we went back over to the bar. After a few minutes, Lisa started to look sick again. She was massaging her temples and complaining of a headache. I asked if she was ready to leave.

"No, not yet. I'm okay. My headache just came back." She tried to remain as normal as possible, but I could tell that she was really sick.

Lisa rested her head on the wall, "Kerri, I don't feel too good. I think I need to go home."

The cars were racing down 9th Street as we crossed the busy intersection. I kept asking Lisa if she was okay. She insisted that it was simply a headache and she just needed to go home and get some rest.

As we crossed the street I joked, "Look out Lisa! Here comes Leo!"

"Where?" she asked frantically.

"Oh, girl, please. Leo ain't thinking 'bout you. It's Saturday night and he is probably on 10th Street making some money."

"Bitch, whatever. Don't even try it! You know his crazy ass be acting a damn fool if I go out, especially with your trifling ass!" she joked.

We exchanged hearty laughs as we got into our ride and drove down E Street then up 12th Street.

All the way home Lisa was stressing about the possibility of running into Leo. "He will kill me if he knew I went out to a club tonight. Please, don't let him be waiting for me outside my building," she prayed aloud.

I was worried about Leo catching Lisa all by herself going into her apartment building so I decided to stay the night with her. At least if I was with her and he tried to attack her, she would have a witness.

As we approached her street Lisa slowed down. She was scared to death. She just knew that Leo would be waiting for her on her doorstep. We drove past the entrance to her apartment building and, once again, slipped through the back door.

Lisa turned to me and said, "This don't make no goddamn sense! This nigga got me scared to come in my own apartment!" We just looked at each other and shook our heads.

Lisa went straight to her bedroom to check her caller I.D. to see if Leo had called. He didn't. She figured that he must have been pulling an all-nighter, trying to make some extra money for her to waste at the mall. She then paged him to let him know that she was okay.

About an hour past and Leo hadn't returned Lisa's page. She still wasn't feeling good so she took a shower and went to sleep. I did the same.

Early that morning Lisa's telephone started to ring. "Hello," Lisa answered the phone in a scratchy, early morning voice.

"What? Who told you that? Let me call you back."

I could hear Lisa talking in my sleep. Then I felt her tugging my arm trying to wake me up, "Kerri, get up!" Lisa nearly shook my arm off my shoulder.

I wiped the stream of slob from the corner of my mouth. "Okay, I'm up. What's the matter?"

"Girl, that was my father. He just called and said that Leo is dead."

"What?"

"I don't know what's going on. I have to find Leo."

At first Lisa was extremely calm. She knew for certain that Leo could not be dead. She had talked to him earlier that night. It just didn't make any sense so she started to beep him again.

We sat on her bed talking, trying to figure out what was going on. She called everybody she could think of that would have known if Leo had really been shot, but she couldn't get any answers. None of them answered their phones.

I tried to keep her calm and sanguine. "Girl, he's okay. You know how niggas be spreadin' rumors and shit."

Though she tried to remain optimistic, deep down inside, she knew it was true.

Lisa had prepared herself for that eventual phone call; the kind that comes at 6:00 in the morning just when you least expect it. The kind where the voice on the other end of the phone sympathetically tells you that the one you love is dearly departed; that his spirit no longer lives in his earthly body and that his heart no longer beats in his manly chest. She knew the type of person Leo was and the type of business he ran. He was a loose cannon that just so happened to sell drugs for a living and she knew that drug dealing loose cannons ended up in one of two places - in prison or in a casket.

After waiting for about an hour for Leo to return her pages, she decided to go look for him. By this time it was about 7:00 in the morning and the sun was just starting to peek from behind the clouds.

We drove to his hang-out spot. It was like a ghost town. There wasn't a lonesome face to be found. We didn't see any yellow police tape laying around so that gave her a little more hope that he was still alive.

We continued to drive around looking for Leo. She hit every spot that he was known to frequent, but Leo was nowhere to be found. Finally after driving around town for about an hour, she started to head back to her apartment.

Lisa turned to me and said, "Kerri, you know I have prepared myself for this day from the moment I fell in love with him. I can't imagine life without him. I love him so much. Please, God, don't let him be dead."

I felt so sorry for her. She was hurting so bad and there was nothing I could do or say to make her feel better. I just kept telling her that it was going to be okay and that we were going to find him.

The mood in Lisa's car was solemn. The radio was turned off and all you could hear was the two of us breathing and the pitiful sound of Lisa's voice mumbling to God to help her find her man.

We turned onto Lisa's street and began to search for a parking space. That's when we both spotted Leo's mother's car easing up the street and that's when Lisa lost it.

She stopped her car in the middle of the street and began screaming, "Oh, no! Kerri, he's dead! He's dead! I know it! Oh God, how could you do this to me!" Lisa was crying uncontrollably. Leo's mother pulled up right beside Lisa's car. With teary eyes and a miserable stare she turned to Lisa and simply shook her head. Leo's mother didn't say anything, she didn't have to, the look on her face said it all.

Lisa continued to cry, scream and curse God for taking Leo away from her. She was in so much pain. I didn't know what to do. Though I felt awful that Lisa was hurting, I couldn't help but feel a little happiness as well. As sympathetic as I was to Lisa's emotional anguish, I was ten times happier that Leo was no longer around to wreck her life.

CHAPTER FIFTEEN

A few months had past and I was still working at the hotel in Virginia. I was planning to move from my uncle's house into my own apartment, but the eleven dollars per hour I was making at the hotel was not enough to live off of.

One day while looking through the Yellow Pages' employment section, I inadvertently stumbled across an ad for an escort agency. "Beautiful Girls . . . Discrete, Confidential, Professional Service." Then I flipped the page and discovered a slew of escort agency ads.

Though I had never before even considered working as an escort, I was curious. I had heard of them, but like most people, I didn't know exactly what an "escort" was.

At first, I thought that escort was just another name for prostitute, but after meeting with some of the girls in the business I learned that it was what you made of it. While the majority of the escorts I talked to did perform sexual favors

in exchange for cash, there were several who didn't. They
all made it clear that you pretty much make your own rules.
If you want to sleep with men for money, so be it. If you
only want to provide companionship or an occasional back
rub or exotic dance, the choice is yours.

     At first I was a bit apprehensive about working as an
escort, but then I gave it more thought and I decided to give
it a try. Since I was working a full-time schedule at the hotel
I decided on three nights a week as an escort. Surprisingly,
it was nothing like I expected. The image I had of perverted
men looking to get laid was all wrong.

     While I did get occasional unimaginable requests
from distorted assholes, the majority of my clients were
older, lonely professional men in search of a pretty face and
a friendly ear. They were usually married, and often in town
on business related trips or attending meetings and
conventions. Most times they would either just want
someone to talk to, bear witness to a sultry lap dance or
perhaps indulge in a soothing massage.

     At $175 per hour, I would take up to three calls on
the weeknights and as many as five calls on a Friday or
Saturday night. Though it was a very lucrative business, I
quit after two months. I had saved up enough money to get
my own place and soon moved from my uncle's house to an
apartment.

     A few months before I moved from Mack's house I
ran into Joanne. I hadn't seen her in about four years, ever
since we had that falling out over Marie and Devin.
Speaking of Devin, I hadn't seen him in about four years as
well. When I got involved with Randall I completely forgot
about Devin. As far as I was concerned he didn't even exist

anymore.

After seeing each other that day we started hanging out again. Though I was still mad at her for betraying me years ago, I am not the type to hold a grudge. My general philosophy is to let bygones be bygones. So with that in mind, it was as if we had never stopped speaking.

Though I had originally planned to be at Mack's house for six to nine months, I managed to accumulate enough money to move in less than three.

My apartment was far from perfect, but it was just what I needed at the time. It was only a few minutes away from both my mother's and grandmother's houses and it was close to shopping centers and schools.

One day as I was parking my car in front of my apartment, I saw Devin. Coincidentally, Joanne was in the car with me. As I was trying to fit into the parking space, Devin came speeding around the corner. When I heard the car screeching closer I nearly broke my neck trying to see who was driving. Unintentionally, Devin and I made direct eye contact. When he realized that I was in the car, he backed up to where my car was sitting.

"Ohmigod! Is that Devin?" I said to Joanne in a state of shock.

"I don't know…it looks like him," she answered.

"It is him! That no good bastard!"

He got out of his car and walked over to me, "Where's Hasannah?" he asked.

"She's right here in the back seat."

"Let me see her, I want to see her," Devin pleaded.

Hasannah was resting quietly in the back of the car when I said, "No. Now is not the time. We need to talk before I let you see her again. Here's my number. Give me a call later so that we can arrange something." He took the number and sped off down the street.

When I said he didn't exist anymore, I really felt that way. When I want to forget about something or someone, I place those feelings and memories in a tiny little box inside my head. As the sole key holder, I lock them up and throw away the key; never thinking of them nor even acknowledging the painful memories again.

That day when I saw Devin, those old feelings I'd tried so hard to erase resurfaced. Suddenly, I felt like that once ingenuous schoolgirl who was not so secretly in love with an upper classman. Though I tried my best to hate him, I didn't. I still cared about him and even had the nerve to get that little butterfly sensation in my abdomen when I heard him speak.

Later that night he called. We hadn't talked in years so we had a lot of catching up to do. He wanted to know why I had taken Hasannah away and why I didn't keep in contact with him when I moved to Georgia. He said that he was shocked to see me, too, and that he didn't even know I was back in town.

I told him that he had given up his parental rights when he refused to take care of Hasannah. He insisted that we had simply experienced a lapse of communication and that he always wanted to provide for Hasannah and loved her very much, but I had taken her away without him knowing her whereabouts. Though most of what he said was true, I did however question his sincerity. After talking for hours on the telephone we agreed to meet the following day.

It was a big day for Hasannah. Though she didn't

remember Devin by face, she always knew his name.
Randall and I had planned to tell her about Devin when she
got older. Since I started dating Randall when Hasannah
was under the age of two, naturally, she started calling
Randall daddy.

Randall was flattered. Though she wasn't his
biological daughter, he treated her like his own. Once we
got married he even tried to legally adopt her, but that plan
fell through when Devin refused to sign the adoption papers.
Three years had passed and Hasannah was now five years
old. She would finally get the chance to meet her real father.

When Devin arrived, Hasannah was excited. She ran
to him and gave him a big hug. He told her how much he
loved her and that he missed her. It was a very touching
scene. Devin took Hasannah to visit his family. When
Hasannah came home she thanked me for letting her see her
father and asked when she would get the chance to see him
again. She was so happy to have finally met him.

Though I was happy for her, I tried not to get caught
up in the moment. I had a sick feeling that he wouldn't stick
around for long so I tried not to let her get too involved.

Just as I had suspected, he kept in contact for a few
months then, slowly but surely, he mysteriously disappeared
and once again became a figment of my imagination.

CHAPTER SIXTEEN

I went to visit Joanne. She was on the phone talking to an old boyfriend, Walter.

When he heard her speak to me he told her to put me on the phone.

"Hey! What's up, Walter?" I asked.

"Aint shit," he answered.

"What you been up to?"

"Nothing, just trynna maintain."

It was good to talk to him. I hadn't seen him in years and was glad to know that he was doing all right. Then, just before I gave the phone back to Joanne, he asked if I knew a guy named Ronnie.

"Ronnie who?"

"Ronnie from uptown."

"Oh yeah, I know him."

He proceeded to tell me that his friend talked about

some girl named Kerri, but he wasn't sure if I was the Kerri his friend spoke of so frequently. When he realized that I was indeed the same Kerri that Ronnie spoke of, he wanted to know if he could get my telephone number to give to Ronnie.

"Sure, tell him to call me."
"Aww man, he's gonna be so happy!" Walter exclaimed.

I was glad to give him my number. I hadn't seen Ronnie since that day we broke up when he caught me riding in Randall's car. A few days later, Ronnie called.
He said that he was glad to talk to me and was dying to see Hasannah. He used to buy her anything she wanted and treated her like family. When he talked to her on the telephone he couldn't believe how much she had grown. The last time he saw Hasannah she was still in diapers and could barely muster a complete sentence.
I had no plans for us to reunite, but I would occasionally pop-up at his house to solicit money from him. Nothing much, just twenty dollars here, fifty dollars there.

We tried for about two weeks to arrange a time that he could come to visit Hasannah, but our schedules were in constant conflict. Then, late one Friday night he called to say that he was in the neighborhood. He asked if he could see her then, but she was already asleep. He said that he didn't care and that he just wanted to look at her and see how much she had grown. He even wanted to give her a kiss good night.
Ronnie had always been a sweetheart. He was the

type of person that everyone loved. Since he was so adamant about seeing Hasannah, I told him to hurry up and come before I changed my mind. A few minutes later he was knocking at the door.

He came in and went straight to Hasannah's bedroom. He pulled the cover down and tucked her in. Then he gave her a kiss on the cheek and closed her door.

We sat in the living room and talked for a few minutes then he reached into his pocket and took out a one hundred dollar bill. "This is for Hasannah." Then he reached into his other pocket and grabbed another one hundred dollar bill, "And this is for your other daughter." He put the money in my hand, gave me a kiss on the cheek and left.

That was Friday night. When I got to work on Monday morning, my voice mailbox was full. My mother had left several messages for me to call her.

When my mother told me what she had just found out I couldn't believe it. *Who in the world would want to kill Ronnie?* I wondered.

He was one of the most likable people on the face of the earth, but somebody obviously didn't like him. He was found late Sunday night shot to death in his car.

CHAPTER SEVENTEEN

I couldn't believe Ronnie was dead. Though we hadn't had much contact in several years, he just seemed like the type of person who would always be around. He always had a kind word to say and would surely brighten up any gloomy day. He was the type of man that women love to hate; loving, caring, affectionate and gullible. He would give his woman anything she wanted and more.

Unfortunately for Ronnie, women don't like nice guys. Women usually have this moronic idea that nice guys are no fun. Just some play thing whose purpose is solely to keep her happy at any and all cost.

As I was trying to rebuild my life and maintain what little sanity I had left, Randall started calling me again.

When I first moved back to D.C. into Uncle Mack's house Randall tried to make amends, but I didn't want to be bothered with him. He kept calling and coming around until he realized that I was really trying to move on with my life. After a while, he got the picture and I didn't hear from him as often.

Then, just as I was getting over him, he weaseled his way back in my life.

Though hopeful, I still didn't trust him. He wasn't drinking as much alcohol as before, but he continued to drink on occasion. I told him that it was either going to be me or the liquor. He chose the liquor.

After that short period with Randall, I didn't date for a while. I was meeting guys left and right, but none of them appealed to me.

By now it was Spring. I hadn't dated in months and was about as "horny" as Earth, Wind and Fire and the Ohio Players put together. I was coming home from a hard day's work when I saw this guy sitting on the front steps of my apartment building.

"Damn, who is that." I wondered.

He was sitting on the steps talking to some people who lived in the building. His sleeveless white T-shirt complimented his ever-so tone upper body. As I walked by I put on my most seductive voice and orchestrated my best baby got back stride. "Hello there," I whispered as I sashayed past him.

He looked up at me, his eyes firmly fixed on my breasts. "Hi, how are you," he said as he opened the door.

I walked up the stairs, turned around to see if he was looking. Needless to say, he was looking.

After seeing him that day, I was determined to get to

know him better. I wouldn't exactly call him handsome, but
he had the perfect body. I wasn't looking for a boyfriend, I
just needed to get laid and from what I saw out there on
those steps, he had all the right equipment.

Come to find out, he lived in the apartment directly
beneath me. His aunt lived in our building on the ground
floor, and he and his mother had just moved into the
complex.

I didn't know much about him, but one thing was for
sure, he was definitely younger than me. Though I had
never before dealt with a younger man, I would surely give
him a try if I could catch his attention.

One day as I was about to come in the building, he
walked outside. He had on another edible sleeveless T-shirt
and his hair was in an afro.

"Damn, what's wrong with your hair" I teased.

"I don't know what's going on with my hair. Do you
cornrow?" he asked.

I wanted so badly to tell him that I had no interest in
his hair. I just wanted to feel his strong hands caressing my
lonesome body.

"Yeah, I can do a little sumpin' sumpin'," I said as I
imagined my round booty gyrating against his masculine
thighs. The sound of him screaming my name put me in a
rhythmic trance as I slowly changed positions so that the
cushion of my ass faced his manly chest. Our bodies
pampered one another and my knees began to quiver. I
could feel every inch of him thrusting my neglected sex
tunnel as he hit it from behind. Just as I was about to
explode with pleasure he tapped me on the shoulder and
asked, "When do you think you can do it? I need it done as
soon as possible."

Shit! I thought to myself. He interrupted my lustful concentration.

I wiped the single bead of sweat from my forehead and said, "Knock on my door in a couple of hours. I might be able to do it then."

The thought of getting my freak on sent cosmic chills up my spine. My nipples were as hard as candy and my insides were dripping with desire.

I desperately wanted to fuck his teenage brains out, but I did not want to do his hair. I just wanted to fuck him and get it over with. When he knocked on my door later that night, I told him it wasn't a good time and that I would let him know when I would be available.

About a week had passed and I had forgotten all about him. Then early one Sunday morning I heard a knock at the door. I was in the kitchen cooking breakfast and talking to Joanne on the telephone. "Who the hell is that knocking on my door 9:00 in the morning," I pondered.

"Girl stop faking. You know it ain't nobody but that guy from downstairs making his daily booty call," Joanne joked.

"Whatever, girl! I don't even know his name," I said while approaching the door. I looked through the peephole and asked, "Who is it?"

"It's Arthur from downstairs. Remember me? You know, the guy who's hair you've been cornrowing for two weeks now," he said sarcastically.

I told Joanne I would call her later.

I unlocked everything but the chain and was extra careful to close my robe partially, just far enough for him to sneak a peek at my fire engine red bra and thong set. I cracked the door open slightly. "So, your name is Arthur."

He took advantage of the peepshow. His eyes

dissected my body as he answered, "Yeah, Arthur, with an A. We never did exchange names. What's yours?"

I licked my lips, ran my hand across my chest and replied, "Kerri, with a K."

I invited him in and offered him some breakfast. After we ate we got into a heated conversation.

"So, do you have a boyfriend?" he asked nosily.

"No, I don't. But I'm married."

"Where's your husband?" Without giving me a chance to comment he continued to question me. "Are y'all separated?"

"Yes, we're separated."

When he learned that I was not in a relationship he asked if he could get to know me better.

"How old are you, Arthur?"

"I'm nineteen," he said with an innocent smile.

"Nineteen? Boy, I'm almost old enough to be your mother!" I joked.

Though I was only twenty-two years old, I could tell that I was much more mature than he was. I was definitely interested in him, but I was a little hesitant because of his age.

I knew he wanted me just as much as I wanted him, so I said, "Arthur, you know you are sexy, don't you?"

He shot me a seductive look. His luscious lips seemed to move in slow motion as he said, "Come here you."

We continued to flirt and give each other compliments until out from nowhere he asked, "Can I be your boyfriend?"

I told him that I was not interested in a relationship, but that I would love to be his sex partner from time to time. When I told him that all I wanted from him was sex he was thrilled.

We agreed that we would be casual sex partners, but that we would be free to see other people. He said that he would not have a problem with that and, in fact, that arrangement was just what he needed. So, with no further ado, we tore each other's clothes off and made wild passionate love right there on the living room floor.

After that first romp with Arthur I was hooked. I couldn't believe that someone his age could give me such a run for my money.

After a couple of months, the novelty wore off. We started seeing each other only one or two nights a week. When I stopped showing interest in him he started getting jealous. Though he said he didn't care if I dated other people, he would become furious whenever I had company over. Since he lived in the apartment directly beneath me he started to watch my every move.

One night I had invited a male friend over. We were in my room watching T.V. when the telephone rang, I answered.

"What's up? What are you doing?" It was Arthur.

"I'm busy right now, can I call you back?"

"Why? Do you have company or something?"

I was so agitated. I sucked my teeth, let out a disapproving sigh and said, "As a matter of fact, I do."

When Arthur hung up the phone I could tell he was mad, but I ignored his irritation and continued to entertain my guest. Then he called again. I didn't answer so he started calling back to back. I overlooked the ringing telephone and told my guest to do the same.

We were trying our damnest to ignore the ringing telephone when all of a sudden we heard a loud noise.

Bam, bam, bam!

"What was that?" My guest was spooked.

Bam, bam, bam!

"There it goes again! Did you hear that?" asked my guest.

I shook my head. "I don't even believe this shit."

At that point my company started to look frightened. He asked me what was going on and I told him not to worry because I had everything under control. Then, I excused myself from the room.

I went into the kitchen and called downstairs to Arthur. I dialed the numbers so hard that the tips of my fingers felt like they were one fire. Arthur answered the phone and I let him have it, "What the fuck is your problem? Why are you banging on the goddamn ceiling?"

"Why aren't you answering your phone?" He snapped.

"Look here, Arthur. You really need to get a grip! I don't understand you! First you claim you don't care if I see other people. Then you start banging on ceilings and shit! If you can't handle our little arrangement, that's fine. We don't have to see each other any more, but don't start pulling that fatal attraction shit on me!" I yelled before slamming the phone.

Arthur called right back. I turned the ringer off.

My guest was so spooked by the whole scene that he made up a cockamamie excuse and got the hell out of Dodge. When he left I turned out the lights and went to bed.

I continued to see Arthur from time to time until I realized he was stalking me.

He would watch the times that I would come and go and as soon as I stepped foot into my apartment, he would call me and leave messages like, "I know you're in there, I can hear you walking around upstairs."

At first, I didn't think anything of it, but then I started to become concerned. He was spending too much time watching me and not enough time minding his own damn business.

I knew that if I had tried to leave Arthur alone gradually he would not have gone quietly. I ended up telling him that my husband and I were getting back together and that I would appreciate it if he would act as if he didn't know me. He was mad at first, but eventually he stopped bothering me.

I had not actually planned to get back with Randall, I was just using that as an excuse to get rid of Arthur.

Eventually, Randall and I did give it one more try. We had been back together for a few weeks when I started to suspect that he was still seeing other people. Though we had both had our share of short lived flings during our separation, I had cut all of my new contacts back when I got back with Randall, but he didn't. He continued to see various female friends and would receive countless pages on his beeper from different girls every day. I was becoming extremely annoyed by his belligerent attempt at outright polygamy so I started to invade his privacy. I would search his pockets for telephone numbers or any other incriminating evidence.

One day I just came out and asked him if he was still

communicating with any of his old female friends. Though
disappointed, his answer did not shock me. He said yes.
Her name was Tammy.

According to Randall, while we were separated, he
had become "good friends" with Tammy and as time went
on, their, as Randall put it, "platonic" relationship blossomed
and he moved in with her.

When Randall came back to D.C. from his two-day
prison term in Georgia his luck had faded. Not only had I
left him and refused to even speak to him, he had
experienced several other set backs.

With his music career utterly stagnant and no
evidence of any clear occupation, he was downright broke.
He didn't have a place of his own to live so he camped out in
his grandmother's attic.

Late one night, in a drunken fit, he took the keys to
his car and hit the road. Feeling lonely and dejected, he
drove around town with no apparent destination. As the
liquor proceeded to captivate his judgment he lost control of
the car. When it was all said and done, he had been arrested
for DWI and his car was totaled. By the time he hooked up
with Tammy he didn't have shit; no money, no car, and not
even a roof over his head.

Tammy had a car and a place of her own so that
scenario worked out just fine for him. He moved himself
and his belongings into her apartment, escaping the
degradation of living in his grandmother's attic.

He would drive around in her car all day while she
worked. With the constant worry of his wife and kids now
gone, he could focus his attention on more important things
like getting money.

Randall, with his pea-brained philosophy, figured that since he and I were separated he had absolutely no responsibility. He thought that since we weren't living together he had no mouths to feed and no backs to clothe. He thought that he was only accountable for himself, so with the fortitude of a power drill and the luck of a four-leaf clover, he assiduously made his financial comeback.

Before long, Randall was once again stacking his money. When his finances were better he came to me to try to patch things up. Still hopeful that he had changed, I decided to give him another chance.

Though he claimed he was not intimate with Tammy, he was still driving her car. Even as we tried to work things out he insisted that he and Tammy were just really good friends and there was no sex involved.

Right around that time my car was stolen. Since neither of us had transportation I began to ignore the fact that he was continuing to use Tammy's car. Though I was pissed off at the entire situation, her car was coming in handy.

In the mornings he would leave my apartment, go to her apartment and pick her up, then drop her off at the subway. From there, he would come back to my apartment, pick me and the girls up, drop them off at the babysitter and drive me to work - in Tammy's car!

I don't know if she was crazy or just plain stupid, but she didn't mind him using her car to drive his wife and kids around.

That went on for a couple of months. Then Randall bought me a car. The only problem was that he was still driving Tammy's car. Using his same excuse, he would try to justify his nonsensical behavior. Though I had never spoken to Tammy and didn't even know what she looked like, I was dying to talk to her. I wanted to know if all he said was true, if they were just good friends and if there was no sex in their relationship.

One day Randall and I had taken a trip to a nearby mall just a few blocks away from my job. I didn't notice it right away, but for some reason he did not want to go to that particular mall. He suggested that we try another mall, but I insisted on that one.

When we arrived at Pentagon City to shop, we first went to BCBG. Randall bought me the cutest outfit. It was a knee length, black fitted skirt with a matching top. Once it was on it looked like a one-piece dress. I found the perfect accessories to match but I needed a pair of shoes.

Randall told me to go to Macy's and pick out one pair of shoes and nothing else. He wanted me to find some shoes quickly and he did not want to look in any other stores.

Though this annoyed me, it didn't raise any questions. Like most men, Randall hated shopping and usually tried to avoid long escapades through overcrowded malls.

After surveying the shoe department at Macys, I decided to try another store. He said he didn't feel like walking through the mall, but I begged him to go with me to Nordstrom.

"Man, I'm not going to no goddamn Nordstrom! You better find some shoes right here or else you won't get any!" he shouted.

Nordstrom was on the opposite end of the mall. Even though I was tired and didn't feel like walking, I begged Randall to give me some more money. "Please, please, please, let me go to Nordstrom. I promise I won't ask you for anything else."

After pleading with him to go with me, he reached into his pocket. "Here's $250! Go your ass to Nordstrom and I'll be waiting for you right here. And hurry up!"

I was so excited at the possibility of finding the perfect pair of shoes that I failed to notice how agitated Randall was.

When we left I reflected back on Randall's conduct at the mall. I didn't know why, but for some reason, I had a sixth sense that he was hiding something. I began to questioned him. "How come you didn't want to go to Pentagon City Mall?"

"I hate that mall. They never have anything I like."

Randall was full of shit. Pentagon City was one of the best malls in the D.C. area and we shopped there frequently. After hearing that outrageous excuse my suspicion grew stronger.

"When did you come to that conclusion? You've been shopping at Pentagon City." I sucked my teeth and waited for an answer.

"Shit, Kerri. Leave me the fuck alone! You got a new outfit and a pair of shoes so shut the fuck up and be happy!"

When Randall started getting defensive with me I knew something was up. I had a feeling that someone was in the mall that he did not want me to see. After giving it more thought it became clear. It was Tammy. It had to be Tammy.

I suspected that she had to have been somewhere in

that mall so I just came right out and asked him, "Was there someone in the mall you didn't want me to see?"

"No. Why would you say that?" He looked guilty as sin.

"Because, you were acting too peculiar, like you were hiding something," I said in a sluethish tone.

"How am I acting peculiar? You should have never asked me to go to the mall with you in the first place. You know I don't like shopping with you because you take too long to figure out what you want. And, furthermore, I just bought you a pair of $300 loafers last week, now all of a sudden you need more shoes! You must think I'm made of money!"

Randall must have thought I was stupid. He knew, that I knew what was going on. But just like a man, he turned the conversation around and made me the topic of discussion.

"First of all, you are the one who mentioned the mall." I recanted. "I had no intention of shopping until you started telling me about some stupid outfit you saw that you thought I would look cute in. Then, when I decided to go to Nordstrom, you nearly lost your mind!"

"That is ridiculous, Kerri. You are just paranoid."

At that point, I knew he was lying because he started to massage the hairs of his goatee. The only time he did that was when he was either nervous about something or lying through his front teeth.

"I ain't paranoid and I sure as hell ain't stupid! Just remember, what's done in the dark is sure to come out in the light and what goes around sooner or later comes back around."

I knew that last statement would do the trick. To a man, the only thing worse than being caught cheating on his wife is the thought of his wife cheating on him.

"Okay, Kerri. If you must know, Tammy works at the mall," he admitted.

"And? So what the fuck! If y'all are such good friends and there is nothing between the two of you, why were you trying to keep me from seeing her?"

"Because I know you. All she would have to do is look at you funny and you'd be ready to kick her ass. What difference does it make anyway? She knows about you and you know about her. There is no need for you to feel threatened, for the last time, Tammy and I are just friends!"

We were so busy arguing that Randall missed his turn. "Damn, Kerri! I wish you would shut up and let me drive. I can't concentrate with all this commotion!"

I remained quiet until he parked.

As we were getting out of the car I rolled my eyes at him. I walked around to his side of the car, looked him dead in the eyes and calmly warned, "Okay, Mr. Motherfucker. You win this time. But I'll tell you one thing, if you want to cheat with Tammy, then I suggest you do so quietly because if I catch you doing something you ain't got no business doing, I'mma kick your black ass." We made direct eye contact. He kissed me softly on the lips and I stormed off.

"Come back here! Why are you trippin'?" Randall asked as he followed me up the stairs to my apartment.

I appeared as calm as the breeze before a storm, but inside I was boiling with anger. I tried my best to remain tranquil, but every time my eyes blinked, I saw flashes of Randall with Tammy.

"Oh, I'm the one who's trippin'? No, motherfucker,

your ass is trippin'! Who do you think you are? Why do you think you can be involved with two people at the same time? In case you forgot, you are still married and I am still your wife! If you are serious about trynna make this thing work, then this shit is gonna have to stop! No ifs, ands or buts about it!"

"Okay, baby. Calm down," he said as he pressed his lips against my forehead. "You know I want our marriage to work. If I have to stop being friends with Tammy in order for us to work things out then that's what I'm gonna have to do."

"I want you to call Tammy right now and tell her that you are bringing her car back to her today!" I demanded.

"Calm down, baby. You are too beautiful to be walking around with that ugly attitude," he said as he squeezed my butt cheeks together like a sandwhich.

"Whatever Randall. Just shut up and call Tammy."

He started to kiss my neck and rub my breast. It was starting to feel good, but I pushed his hand and moved away. "Randall, I'm serious. Call her right now."

"Okay, baby. I'll call her in a minute," he whispered as he stuck his tongue in my ear lobe.

Randall was persistent. He was feeling me up and I was falling for every minute of it. His barrage of kisses and touches lured me into the bedroom. Forty minutes and four orgasms later, our naked bodies lay stretched across the mattress in a pool of sweat.

The next day, Randall supposedly called Tammy and told her that he couldn't see her anymore. He said that he was going to return her car in a couple of days, just as soon as he went to the dealer to buy one for himself.

As much as I wanted to believe him, I knew he was lying. He swore he had severed all ties with Tammy, but I knew better. Two weeks had passed and he was still driving her car.

CHAPTER EIGHTEEN

Talking to Randall was like talking to a brick wall. I knew he still hadn't said anything to Tammy about returning her car.

Frustrated that Randall was still communicating with Tammy, I decided to pay her a visit. I didn't know much about her, just her name and where she worked. I didn't have her phone number, but I did copy her address off of a piece of mail I saw in her car one day.

That night I drove to her apartment complex. Not sure which unit she lived in, I patiently waited in my car outside of her apartment building. The piece of mail I had copied her addressed from failed to indicate the apartment number. After waiting for about an hour, there was no sign of her so I left.

By the time I got home, I was even more frustrated. I saw Tammy's red Ford Escort parked outside of my apartment building so I knew Randall was home.

When I went in the house, I went straight to bed and didn't say a word to Randall.

The next day, I couldn't focus on anything. I had a stack of work waiting for me on my desk and my boss was getting on my last nerve. I was still working at the same hotel, which just so happened to be a few blocks away from the mall where Tammy worked.

Mad as hell and desperately seeking answers, I left work early. I circled the mall several times contemplating whether or not to confront Tammy. Finally, I decided to go home.

Later that evening I couldn't fight the curiosity any longer. I decided to drive back to the mall and find out what was really going on.

When I first walked into Nordstrom my initial reaction was to turn back around and pretend that Tammy didn't exist. Like I had done so many times before, I tried to put her in that same tiny little box in my head that almost every unpleasant thought I had ended up, but she wouldn't cooperate.

No matter how hard I tried to ignore her presence, she remained visible. Day in and day out, all I could think about was who is this Tammy and what does she want with my husband. Angry and confused, I meticulously searched each department of the store looking for her.

Since I had no idea what Tammy looked like I went to every register with a woman behind the counter. Starting on the top floor, I walked up to each female cashier and said, "Hi, I'm looking for a girl that works here by the name of

Tammy. Would you happen to be her?"

I must have asked that question twenty times before I had a brainstorm. *Since Randall didn't want me to buy shoes from Nordstrom, I'll bet she works in the shoe department.* I thought to myself.

The shoe department was on the first floor and I was on the second so I hopped on the elevator and hurried down the hall to the shoe section.

Just as I was about to ask the gentleman behind the counter if Tammy worked in the shoe department, a young lady appeared from the back of the store. Without giving much thought to what I would say, I blurted out, "Hi, I'm Kerri. Are you Tammy?"

She turned to me and said, "No I'm not, but she works in the jewelry department."

I thanked her for the help and rushed to the jewelry section.

Before walking up to the counter I cased the scene. There was a light skinned black girl with a short hair cut behind the register. *Look at this bitch. That's got to be her* I thought to myself.

I stood still for a moment to process my thoughts. Though my initial gut feeling was to walk up to her and slap the taste out of her mouth, the last thing I wanted to happen was to be arrested in the state of Virginia. Since I had been arrested for shoplifting and had a police record, Virginia was the last place on earth I wanted to start some trouble. With the poise of a princess and the heart of a soldier, I walked up to her and said, "Excuse me, would you happen to be Tammy?"

She informed me that she was not Tammy, but that Tammy was scheduled to be in at 6:00. I looked at my watch. It was 5:45.

I thanked the saleslady and walked over to the sitting area in the shoe section. I chose that spot because it allowed me to see people entering the store from three different angles. One angle displayed people entering from the mall, another angle displayed people entering the store from the garage and another displayed people coming down the escalator. Before I could make myself comfortable, I noticed a little red hatch-back pull up to the door at the garage entrance. I wasn't sure if it was Tammy's car, but it looked exactly like hers.

I was sitting on the courtesy couch, straining to see who was getting out of the tiny red Ford. Then I noticed that a man was driving. As I looked more closely I recognized Randall's face. He was dropping Tammy off for work.

As I sat on the couch trying to remain calm, she walked through the door. *Oh, I don't even believe this shit* I said to myself as she walked bye.

Unknowingly, she had just walked past her boyfriend's wife. Though she wasn't as slim as I was, and she could have used a few lessons in Fashion 101, she had a cute face and looked an awful lot like me. I was too through.

I sat there on that couch in a state of shock. Not only did Randall have the nerve to fuck with a girl that looked like me, but she had his name tattooed on her arm just like the one I had.

I watched her put her things away, and when the other saleslady left, I walked up to her register.

"Hi. Can I talk to you for a second?" I asked.

She must have thought I was a customer. "Sure, is

there something I can help you with?"

"Yes, there is, actually. First, let me start by saying that there is no need to be alarmed, but I am Kerri, Randall's wife. I would like to talk to you." Though I was furious, I tried to maintain my composure so that I could get as much information as possible.

"Okay, no problem. Where do you want to talk?" She asked.

"Right here is fine with me. Can you talk right now? I mean, if you're busy, I can come back. I'm not here to start any trouble, I just want some answers."

"Now is fine. So, what is it that you would like to know?"

"What has Randall told you about me and him?" I wanted to find out how much she knew and how much of what she knew was true.

"He pretty much just said that he was married and that you all were separated. To be honest, Kerri, he's been very straight forward with me."

"Well, did he tell you that we were back together and, that right now, he's back living with me?"

"He mentioned that you all were thinking about getting back together, but, no, I wasn't aware that you all were actually together again."

We talked for about thirty minutes, come to find out Randall had been lying just as I'd suspected. I thanked Tammy for taking the time to talk to me and then I left.

The speed limit sign read 60 mph, I was pushing 100. I couldn't wait to get home. After hearing what Tammy had to say I was furious. Even though I never really believed him when he said that they were just good friends, part of me wanted to trust him.

Tammy called him as soon as I left the store so by the time I got home he was waiting for me.

When I came in the house he had the nerve to have a bogus attitude with me. He walked up to me and started screaming, "You are so stupid! Why would you go out there and make a fool out of yourself?"

"First of all, I'm the one who should be yelling! Second of all, I didn't make a fool out of myself and I refuse to let you make a fool out of me either!" I yelled.

"I can't believe you went to her job! You must be the dumbest woman on the face of the earth! Why would you believe anything Tammy told you? You know I don't fuck with her like that!"

"I hope you got what you were looking for!" I teased.

"You are nuts! Who am I with right now? Who did I marry? I don't want Tammy's fat ass and she knows it! That's why she told you all those lies because she knows I don't want her!"

"Look here, Randall, I am sick of your shit! Pack your bags and get the fuck out!" I demanded.

"Oh, so it's like that now? You just gonna kick me out? Just like that, huh?" He was trying to convince me to listen to his side of the story.

"I sure am, now get your shit and go! I want you out of here, now!" I yelled.

"Can we at least talk about it?" he begged.

"Talk about it? Talk about what? I'm not gonna tell you no goddamn more, get your shit and get the fuck out! Take your dirty dick ass back to Tammy because I don't need this shit! Triflin ass mutherfucker! I hate you! Get the fuck out of my house!" I was livid.

After a grossly unsuccessful showcase of emotions, Randall packed his bags and left. I didn't hear from him again for weeks.

When Randall left my house that time I was befuddled. Though common sense eventually prevailed, the combination of my need for financial assistance and my unwarranted love for him was tugging at my good judgment. He would call me several times a day. Each call ended with a violent display of hurtful words, usually my own. But on one day in particular, I made a call to him out of complete desperation.

I was at work when I received a phone call from Arthur's mother. She was home from work that day and had heard someone walking around in my apartment. Knowing that I had already left for work, and fearing that my house was being burglarized, she called me. I told her to call the police and that I would be there shortly. As I was getting ready to leave my job she called again. She told me that she had seen who was upstairs in my apartment, it was the management staff.

They were there with an eviction notice and the manager said that if I wasn't home in fifteen minutes with $2,000 of so called "back rent," my belongings would be placed outside on the sidewalk.

When I arrived, the apartment manager was sitting in my living. *Ain't this about a bitch. This motherfucker has got more nerve!* I thought to myself. "What seems to be the problem?" I asked.

"Well, Mrs. Mitchell, according to our records, you owe us $2,000."

"Two thousand dollars my ass! I don't owe y'all

shit! I pay my rent on time every month! I don't know what
type of games y'all playing, but y'all better stop fucking
with me. I have never missed a rent payment and I have all
my receipts to prove it!"

He went on to explain that I had moved in on a
"special" and that, even though they advertised the two
bedroom apartment for $695, that was only for the first
month. Each month thereafter the rent was $995 and since I
had been paying only $695, I owed them money.

He asked if I had received the court notices that were
left on my door.

I told him that when I saw those notices I threw them
in the trash because I was paying the rent I had agreed to.
Though we disagreed on the amount I owed them , if any, he
insisted that if I couldn't come up with the $2,000 he would
have no other choice than to proceed with the eviction.

Since I didn't have any cash on hand I called
Randall. Even though we weren't speaking, I knew he
would give me the money.

I was grateful that Randall brought me the money,
but I was pissed-off at myself for not having any money
saved up. Randall, on the other hand, didn't mind at all. In
fact, that shit just made his day.

After that incident we started speaking and before
long, we were an item again.

Before I decided to let Randall move back in with
me, I wanted to make sure that Arthur understood that
Randall and I were back together. At first Arthur seemed
upset, but after a while he appeared to be okay with it.

Randall and Arthur would run into each other in the
hallway and they would speak. Nothing heavy, just "Hey,
what's up?" and stuff like that. Arthur and I played it off so

well that Randall never suspected that I had been knocking boots with Arthur. It was all going according to plan until the day I moved out.

I didn't tell Arthur that I was moving. To be honest, I thought he was over me, but I would soon find out just how much "in love" with me he really was.

Since I didn't tell anyone I was moving I didn't have a pre-arranged babysitter. Knowing that my mother wasn't available, I asked Arthur's aunt who also lived in our building to keep an eye on the girls while we moved. She said okay and I sent them downstairs to her apartment.

I decided to go downstairs to check on the girls while Randall, my two uncles and my cousin were getting my stuff packed on the truck.

Arthur's aunt and I were sitting at her dining room table when the telephone rang. Since I was the closer to the phone she told me to answer it. "Hello," I said to the caller.

"Who is this?" asked the caller.

"Who is this?" I asked in return.

Even though I knew it was Arthur, I pretended that I did not recognize his voice.

"Man, put my aunt on the phone!" he demanded.

A few minutes later Arthur was knocking at her door. He wanted to know if she had a cigarette. She invited him back to her bedroom. I was preparing to go back upstairs when he walked past the dining room and said, "I hate that bitch!"

I just looked at his aunt and burst into an infectious roll of laughter. "What's his problem?" I asked her.

"Girl, I don't know what you did to my poor nephew, but he is trippin'."

I went back upstairs to help pack. Then all of a sudden I heard some commotion downstairs. Randall was so busy packing that he didn't hear anything at first.

I stepped into the hallway and heard someone yell, "Stop, Arthur! Put the knife down!"

Then, someone else yelled, "Stop him! Don't let him get upstairs!"

I didn't know exactly what was going on, but I knew it wasn't good. From what I gathered out there in that hallway, Arthur was trying to get upstairs to me.

I ran back in my apartment and locked the door. I didn't know what was going on in Arthur's head, but I knew he was out to get me.

I was so afraid. Even though I could hear all the commotion downstairs and I could hear his family trying to hold him down, I was more afraid of Randall finding out about my sexual escapades than with Arthur doing any harm to me.

Still not fully aware of the psychotic stage show that was taking place in Arthur's apartment downstairs, I went into the bathroom and closed the door. I sat on the edge of the bathtub and started to cry. Then I got down on my knees and started to pray, "Please Lord, just let me get through this one time, I promise I'll be good." I begged and pleaded with God to "Get me through this...." I was so scared. I vowed that if I made it through that day alive, I wouldn't sleep with anymore strangers no matter how good they looked in a sleeveless T-shirt.

When I came out of the bathroom almost everything had been packed up and placed on the moving truck. Randall and one of my uncles were making fun of all the

commotion that was going on downstairs. "Somebody don'
turned that young nigga the hell out!" One of my uncles said.
"Yeah, he's off the hook!" joked another.
Randall even commented on Arthur's antics.
Somebody had turned Arthur out all right, but what
none of them knew was that somebody was me.

After about thirty minutes, Arthur's mother had
called the police. We heard the sirens as they approached
the apartment complex. I looked out the window to see what
was going on and I couldn't believe what I saw. There were
about three or four police cruisers, an ambulance and a fire
truck.
Then I saw Arthur being escorted out of the building
wearing a white straight jacket.
What the fuck? I thought to myself.

I went back into the hallway to try and eavesdrop as
Arthur's mother was telling the police what had happened.
"So, Ma'am, what happened here today?" the officer
asked.
Arthur's mother looked worn out, "It's my son. He is
so stupid. He's been fucking with this girl upstairs. She
went back to her husband and now he wants to kill
everybody!"
"Wait a minute. How do you know your son wants
to kill someone?" the officer asked.
"Because he said so. He grabbed a butcher knife out
of the kitchen and was headed upstairs when I stopped him.
I just don't know what to do with him. He was so fixated on
killing that girl that when we tried to restrain him, he went
crazy! He started destroying my apartment. He kicked the

furniture around, punched holes in the walls and punched me in the mouth by accident. I've never seen him this way before. I mean, even my boyfriend who is twice his size couldn't hold him down. When he realized we were not going to let him out of this apartment, he tried to cut his own throat! I want him to get some help. I don't know what to do with him."

Just as I was listening in on their conversation I saw Randall approaching the apartment building. "Oh God, please don't let them say anything to Randall," I prayed.

When Randall walked in the building, they all got quiet. I ran back into the apartment and was pretending once again to be using the bathroom, but I was really trying to get my story straight. I was certain that by now Randall was on to me. I just knew that he had figured it all out. Much to my delight, he still didn't have a clue.

"C'mon, Kerri. We're done. We're just waiting on you," he said.

"Okay. Go ahead, I'm right behind you," I assured Randall.

I waited until the coast was clear. When the ambulance pulled off with Arthur in the rear cabin, I grabbed my purse and headed for the door. As I walked past the police and Arthur's mother she said, "There she is officer...that little slut. It's all her fault!"

Though I was terribly embarrassed and I did feel somewhat responsible, I just kept walking.

So with my best baby got back strut, I rested one hand on my hip, threw my head up in the air and walked right out of that building just as if nothing ever even happened.

CHAPTER NINETEEN

Crestwood Luxury Apartments, with it's suburban address, wall to wall carpet, two full baths and in-unit personal laundry, was every low-income Southeast resident's dream. But, as luck would have it, my one year, $1,000 a month lease eventually turned into a court ordered writ. Or, in Layman terms, I would soon be evicted.

After spending a grand total of thirty days in our new apartment Randall was at it again. But this time it wasn't his drinking that tore us apart, it was his ongoing affair with Tammy.

Every day we would argue over his whereabouts and why he didn't come home the night before. It got so bad that he stopped denying it. He pretty much told me that he *was* still seeing her and that if I didn't like it *I* could leave *his* apartment. I responded by telling him that the apartment was in my name he would be the only one leaving.

Moving into that expensive apartment was one of the dumbest moves I ever made. I only moved there because it was where Randall wanted to live. He was going to pay the rent and I was going to save my money. I had fixed my pay stubs to read that I made twice as much as my actual salary so that we could qualify for the apartment, but I should have listened to my intuition. I knew that Randall and I couldn't last five seconds together, let alone "one year" as the lease required. But once again, I ignored my thoughts and let my foolish heart and greedy hands lead the way.

Randall didn't waste any time. By the next day all of his stuff was gone. He had officially moved out. And to make matters worse, I had just found out that I was pregnant…again.

The following two weeks were a combination of breakdowns and letdowns. Randall insisted that he didn't want me to have the baby because he suspected that I was cheating. Some guy that I had been friends with told Randall that he slept with me. Randall used that as his basis for continuing his affair with Tammy.

Though I didn't really want to have another baby, I was hurt by the way Randall responded to that pregnancy. He did not want me to have the baby and he refused to pay for the abortion. Since he believed that I had slept with another man, he insisted that I pay for my own abortion.

After that pregnancy was terminated I went into a state of depression. Not only had Randall left me, I was now facing an eviction. I was in so much of a rut that I didn't go to work for a whole week. A few days later, I quit my job.

The day of my scheduled eviction I met a guy at a

nearby McDonald's. His name was Stevie. Our eyes met as I walked into the McDonald's and he stood in the line directly beside me. He spoke to me first.

After introducing himself, we exchanged phone numbers. He said that if I were up to it, he would like to take me out to dinner. As we exited the restaurant, I couldn't help but notice his shiny black Mercedes-Benz with slightly tinted windows.

My first impression of Stevie was that he was harmless, just a horny older man with a pocket full of money. He had accomplished everything in life he had set out to do. He owned a nice home in a prestigious neighborhood and he had his own business. He even drove a nice luxury car. But despite all of his success, he was still not happy. He had obtained tremendous material wealth, yet he had no one to share it with.

Thanks to Stevie, my belongings were never thrown out on the street. He rented a U-haul moving van and moved my belongings into my aunt's basement.

I made arrangements to stay with my aunt for six months. She had a five-bedroom house and lived there all alone. But those six long months turned into six short weeks. I dealt with her unreasonable house rules for as long as I could stand and then I hit the pavement in search of a place of my own.

CHAPTER TWENTY

In an effort to make a better living for myself, I conjured up a magnificent scheme that ensured me a salary twice that of which I was accustomed.

I had found the perfect two-bedroom apartment in Bowie, Maryland. It was just as nice as Crestwood Apartments, but about one hundred dollars cheaper. There was only one problem. I was working as a temp and not making a lot of money.

I started to survey job titles in the Help Wanted ads. The majority of the higher paying salaries required a college degree. Though I had taken some college courses, the only degree I held was a metaphorical Ph.D. in Life Experience. Unfortunately for me, most employers did not acknowledge that as a preferred credential.

So I had to choose a career of which I either had extensive experience or technical knowledge.

I was lacking in experience, but I knew computers. The combination of my software expertise and typing speed of 80 words per minute, led me to the job title of legal secretary.

Before that moment, the thought of working for a law firm had never crossed my mind. But when I began to see ad after ad for legal secretaries offering starting salaries in the forty-thousands, my brain started working overtime.

I had all the technical skills that were required of the job, I just didn't have the experience. I knew that in order for me to land the perfect job at one of the top law firms I would have to have a legal background.

Then I had an idea. What if I were to create a bogus Law Firm: meaning I would get an additional telephone line turned on in my apartment, leave a very convincing professional message on the voice mail system and provide my own employment reference and verification.

It sounded like a bit much, but considering half of the stunts I had pulled over the years, I was sure I could pull this one off as well.

So, not long after I moved into my new two-bedroom apartment, I created the counterfeit law firm of Woodner, Katz & Bothel.

I didn't know Woodner, had never met anyone by the name of Katz and couldn't even begin to tell you who Bothel was, but it sure sounded like the name of a prestigious law firm if you asked me. I called the telephone company to have them set up an additional line in my apartment. They informed me that since I already had several of the advanced features on my telephone line, I was entitled to a second telephone number free of charge. It was not an additional telephone line, just a different telephone number with a distinctive ring or identi-ring as it was known.

Since most businesses had telephone numbers that ended in 00, I requested that my identi-ring number end in 00 as well. That was no problem.

This was the immaculate resolution to my dilemma. Not only did I have a second telephone number, but the indenti-ring number also came with it's very own private voice mailbox. I set the voice mailbox up as follows: "Hello. You have reached the law firm of Woodner, Katz & Bothel. We are unavailable to take your call at the moment, but if you would leave a detailed message, someone will return your call as soon as possible. Thank you." And with that, a legal secretary was born.

I created a resume straight from heaven. I claimed to have been a legal secretary at Woodner, Katz & Bothel for seven years. I had a home office complete with computer, fax machine and everything else I needed to get my career off in the right direction. I instructed Hasannah and Randa to "Never answer mommy's telephone when it rings."

When I started to fax my resume around town I would get responses within minutes. I was sure to use my mother's D.C. address and (202) area code telephone number on my resume. That way, when filling out job applications, I would use my actual Maryland address and (301) area code telephone number as my employment information.

Within the first week, I had more than ten interviews scheduled. After the interviews, I would call home to check my identi-ring's voice mailbox and retrieve the messages that were left by potential employers.

I would return their calls, transform my voice to that of a professional women and pretend to be Mrs. Such and

Such, the Office Administrator with Woodner, Katz & Bothel. A couple of times I even pretended to be an attorney with the firm. I would answer all of their questions and give myself a glowing reference. By the time I was through with the call I would have the job in my back pocket. It was so easy. I couldn't believe how naïve those so-called professionals were.

Within no time I had landed my first gig as a legal secretary. It was with a small law firm and I was offered a starting salary of $38,000. I knew that I could have gone to a bigger firm and gotten more money, but since I didn't know what to expect I figured that starting with a small firm was my best bet. Besides, considering that only four months earlier I was making a grand total of $22,000 a year as a Hotel Sales Assistant, $38,000 didn't sound so bad after all.

CHAPTER TWENTY·ONE

Things had finally started to turn around for me. I had a nice apartment in a good neighborhood, a great job and a generous male friend to provide that something extra every woman needs in her life. Though we were not officially exclusive, Stevie was pretty much the only person I was seeing at the time.

After a while I realized that he wanted more from our relationship than I was willing to give. He tried his best to win me over with monetary rewards, but I grew tired of his desperate attempts to capture my appeal.

One day Joanne had come over to my place to visit. We decided to go to T.G.I.Friday's for dinner. Though I had plenty of cash, I didn't want to spend my own money so I called Stevie and asked to use his credit card instead. He said sure, but I had to come by his house to pick it up.

We drove to Stevie's house to get the credit card then to the restaurant.

After eating, Joanne informed me that a couple of guys we knew wanted to come over to my place to hang out later. I didn't see anything wrong with that so I said okay.

When we got back to my place, Joanne called the guys and before long they were knocking at the door. Joanne and I were entertaining our guests when the telephone rang. "Hello," I said while laughing at something Joanne had said.

"What's up, baby?" It was Stevie.

As soon as I heard his voice my mood changed. My voice got unenthusiastically low and my eyes rolled so far into the back of my head that they almost got stuck. "Oh...hey, what's up?" I said while pretending to gag myself with my index finger.

"Nothing much, just wondering what time you were coming back over here."

Puzzled, I asked, "Who said I was coming over there?"

"You did, right after you took my credit card off the coffee table."

"No, what I said was I'll be back. I didn't say when."

"Well...I took that as you saying you'll be back when you finished eating. So what time should I be expecting you?"

Just then, Joanne yelled from the living room, "Hey Kerri, John wants to know what you have in here that smells so good."

"Who was that?" Stevie asked.

"Nobody."

"Who was that? Do you have company?"

"Yes, as a matter of fact I do. Can I call you back when they leave?"

"Kerri, who was that? Do you have a man in your house?"

"What difference does it make if it's a man or a woman?"

Stevie hung up the phone.

I went back into the living room and finished entertaining my guests. John asked if I would ride with him to the liquor store to get some drinks and snacks.

On our way to the store John and I started talking about men and women in relationships.

"John, why do men feel the need to control their relationships with women?"

"Not all men are like that, Kerri."

"Whatever. Every man I've dealt with is like that."

"That's because you attract assholes," he said with a snide chuckle.

"Damn, you hit that shit right on the nozzle. But why?"

"Why what?"

"Why do I attract nothing but knuckleheads?"

He shot me a look that said if I didn't know by then, I would never know so I quickly changed the subject.

On our way back to my place, I started thinking about Stevie. *Why was he trippin'...we never agreed to be exclusive, so why did he care who was at my place?* He really surprised me when he hung up the phone, that seemed childish.

Back at my apartment complex we searched for a parking space. John grabbed the drinks while I snatched the bag of goodies. We had some of everything, chips, candy, nuts, and a pound of sweet and sour Gummy Patch Kids.

We were walking up to my building when all of a sudden I heard a loud, obnoxious voice exclaim, "Uh huh! I caught you!" Stevie popped out of his Mercedes like a Jack in the Box.

"What is your problem?" I asked.

"What do you mean 'What is my problem?' I have been at my place waiting for you for the past three hours!"

"And?" I was not feeling that shit he was talking.

"So is this why you couldn't find your way to my house? Is this your new boyfriend or something?"

"Don't worry about who he is. Why are you sitting out here spying on me?"

John kept walking in front of us. He couldn't have cared less about Stevie and the infantile scene he was making.

"Well, I'll tell you what…just let me get my charge card and you and your little friend can finish whatever it is that y'all were doing."

I followed John into the building and Stevie followed me. The three of us were standing in the hallway in front of my door when I realized I didn't have my keys. "Shit! I forgot my keys!" I began banging on the door.

When Joanne opened the door she was cackling like a wild hyena. She was laughing so hard that she almost choked on her own saliva. "Girl, that damn maniac keeps calling here looking for you. I told his pressed ass that you were gone and he kept calling back asking me where you were at and I told him-"

Stevie cut her off mid sentence. "Well that damn maniac is standing right here and I just wanna get my charge card and go my pressed ass back home!"

Joanne didn't know that Stevie was behind me and she was surprised to see him standing there. She quickly opened the door and flew in the back to my bedroom and shut the door.

"I just wanna get my shit and go. Hurry up!" Stevie demanded.

"Don't rush me!" I yelled as I reached into my purse to get his credit card.

"You don't have to worry about me anymore, I'm through with you. Don't ever call me again!" He snatched his credit card from my hands and stormed out the door.

"Halleluah! Can I get a witness!" I yelled. I slammed the door so hard that the pictures on the wall shook and fell to the floor. I couldn't believe Stevie. The nerve of him.

I wasn't mad that he didn't want to see me anymore, I was mad because he beat me to the punch. He gave me my walking papers before I had a chance to give him his.

I was determined not to let him have the last word so I ran to the window, stuck my head out and yelled, "And the next time you think about sneaking up over here stalking me and shit, you'd better think twice...pencil dick motherfucker!"

He flipped me the birdie then got in his Benz and sped off.

Joanne clowned me so bad for that comedic scene with Stevie. However, I didn't think it was all that funny. Not only had he violated my space by showing up at my apartment unannounced, he embarrassed me in front of my friends. Then he had the nerve to play big and call himself dumping me.

I couldn't win for losing. Whenever I tried to give a man a chance this is the type of bullshit I had to deal with. The men I managed to hook myself up with were either too possessive, too controlling, or just plain ole' fucked up in the head.

The constant question I found myself asking was *Am I ever gonna find a good man?* And the constant answer I came up with was *Hell no. Not in this lifetime.*

CHAPTER TWENTY-TWO

It was now springtime again. I was still working at the same law firm, but it was no longer exciting to me. I had been missing days left and right and contemplating whether to quit or stay.

Joanne had been going through problems at her apartment. She was so busy shopping at expensive stores buying fashionable tokens for her wardrobe, that she couldn't keep up with her monthly rental payments.

According to Joanne, she had fallen so far behind in payments that she willingly broke her lease agreement in an effort to save money. I later discovered that she wasn't trying to save money, she was being evicted.

Before the authorities came to set her stuff out, she fled the apartment and moved in with her cousin. But that split decision turned out to be a grave mistake.

According to Joanne, her cousin was impossible to get along with. Joanne's cousin must have felt the same way about her because, approximately two weeks after Joanne moved in, she came home to find that the locks had been changed.

When Joanne called and told me that she had nowhere to go, I offered to let her stay with me for a few weeks until she got herself together. The original plan was for her to stay at my place for no more than a month while she looked for an apartment.

At first she was sleeping in the living room, but after a month had past and she was still there, we discussed the possibility of her renting Hasannah and Randa's bedroom.

We both agreed that since she didn't have any furniture, aside from her bed and T.V., that $300 a month would suffice.

My rent was $900. Although I was making good money and had no problem paying rent on time, the extra $300 would come in handy. Besides, even when Joanne had her own place she spent so much time at my apartment that it was like she practically already lived there.

So we borrowed my Uncle Mack's pick-up truck and moved her things into the kids' bedroom. The closet in the kids' bedroom and the hall closet were large enough to hold the kids' beds, dresser and toys, so we packed their stuff away and Hasannah and Randa began sleeping in my bedroom.

I enjoyed having Joanne there for the first couple of months. We would find all kinds of mischief to get ourselves into and my place had become a hot place to hang out.

Late one evening I received a call from my mother. She told me that Randall had been in a car crash and that his Acura TL had been totaled. He was in the hospital unconscious.

Though I probably should have been concerned about Randall's well being, I couldn't have cared less. Since his car was in my name and paid in full, the only thing I was concerned with was contacting the auto insurance company so that I could collect the money. After all, the car legally belonged to me.

The next day I stayed home from work and went to the junk yard where the car had been transported so that I could get a vehicle release clearance. After I obtained all the paperwork I needed I went to the insurance company.

"Sorry, Mrs. Mitchell, but you are no longer insured with Allstate," the man behind the desk said.

I walked out of that insurance company mad as hell. Randall was even more stupid than he looked. Apparently, he had let the policy lapse. He made the first month's payment and hadn't sent a payment since. All the money he spent on that car was a waste. I just shook my head, got into my car and drove back home.

That week both Joanne and I had stayed home from work. We hung out all day and stayed up all night. We were so busy goofing off and having fun that we had completely forgotten about our jobs.

I don't know how I came up with the idea, but I told my boss that my husband had died in a car crash. Maybe it was because I didn't want to go back to work and I figured that if I told my job that my husband had died, I could stay home with pay for at least two more weeks.

Just as I thought, I was given two weeks bereavement leave. Randall was not actually dead, he was in the hospital in a state of unconsciousness. When he came out of his temporary coma, the police arrived with an arrest warrant.

The night of his accident, Randall had been drinking. The police where trying to pull him over for speeding, but when he saw the flashing lights and heard the sirens he tried to make a run for it. The police was tailing Randall's Acura as he tried to speed around a sharp ben. By the time the police made it to the other side they didn't see Randall. His car had disappeared.

According to the accident report, as the police were about to go in the opposite direction, they noticed what looked like a car's headlights beaming through a dense patch of bushes.

Sure enough, it was Randall's Acura. He had driven through a barricade of bushes and his car landed upside down, completely submerged in a murky pond.

Luckily for him the police were already at the scene. Had they not been, he would have died for sure.

So, after waiting for Randall to gain consciousness, the police were there to take him off to jail for DWI, Wreckless Endangerment, Fleeing the scene and a host of other related charges.

I was still at home so-called grieving, when I received a call from the operator. "You have a collect call from Randall Mitchell, an inmate at the Prince George's County Jail. Do you accept the charges?"

"Hell no!" I told the operator.

Who did Randall think he was? I hadn't seen or heard from him since he packed his shit up and left me stranded in that high ass apartment that he knew I could not afford.

If he thought I was going to come running to his
rescue he had better think again. *I'll show his ass* I thought
to myself as I called the telephone company to request a
block on collect calls. Just then, I heard a knock at the door.

"Who is it?" I asked as I looked through the
peephole.
"A delivery for Mrs. Mitchell."

I opened the door and signed for the beautiful
bouquet of spring flowers.
My face lit up like a Christmas Tree. "Ohmigod, who
could these be from?" I was so excited.
"Maybe they're from Stevie or perhaps the guy I
went to lunch with the other day," I told Joanne.

I opened the tiny envelope and read the card, "Sorry
for your loss. I hope these flowers brighten your day, with
deepest sympathy." The flowers had been sent by my boss.

I had conjured many tales before, but having my boss
believe that my husband was dead was definitely un-called
for. I cracked a devilish smile and nearly died laughing.
Though I would have loved for Randall to have remained
locked up, he was eventually released from jail.

CHAPTER TWENTY-THREE

By now, it was the beginning of winter. Joanne and I had moved into a larger apartment. After six months of having the kids in my bedroom I was on the verge of a nervous breakdown. I couldn't take having them in my intimate space any longer so I transferred to a three-bedroom apartment a few buildings away.

When Joanne initially moved in we didn't have any problems. But after a while, I became annoyed by some of Joanne's habits. For instance, Joanne was a smoker. I repeatedly told her not to smoke marijuana in my apartment, but she would sneak and do it anyway when I wasn't home.

Before she moved in, I explicitly expressed my concern over the issue. I knew that she was an avid weed smoker, so I told her that I would not allow smoking of any kind in my apartment and that if such an arrangement would be a problem for her, she would have to look elsewhere for a place to call home. She agreed to the no-smoking rule and broke it every chance she got.

Then there was the issue over household items. I would always stock up on things like soap, laundry detergent and toilet paper. I didn't have a problem with her using anything of mine, all I asked was that when we started to run low on any particular item, that one of us replenish the supply. The problem with that request was, nine times out of ten, I was the only one replenishing the supply. She would use her fill of everything in the apartment, but when it came time to restock, she would not contribute a penny to the shopping fund.

There were several other "little" things that annoyed me about Joanne, but I tried my best to keep them to myself.

Then one day, a few days after Christmas, my cousin Tony paid me a visit. Before he left he handed me an envelope that belonged to Joanne. He said that he had found the envelope laying in the hall and that it was already opened when he picked it up. Come to find out, the envelope contained a paycheck she had been waiting on.

When I gave her the envelope she went off on me. She accused me of opening her mail and deliberately holding her check. I told her that she had it all wrong, that I had just gotten her check from my cousin and that it was already opened when he found it in the building hallway across from the mailboxes.

We ended the conversation and she went into her bedroom and shut the door. I assumed that everything was okay so I did the same. Thirty minutes later a police officer was knocking at the door. I opened the door and asked what he was there for and he said that he was responding to a complaint of mail fraud. Joanne had called herself reporting me for allegedly opening her mail. I was hot with anger.

Joanne escorted the officer to her bedroom and shut the door. I couldn't hear what was being said, but after about five minutes or so I knocked on her bedroom door and asked what was going on.

The officer had taken her complaint and then asked me my side of the story. He made a record of the details of my description of what had happened then he left.

That was the straw that broke the camel's back. She had to go. I was convinced that Joanne was completely off her rocker. I knew that if I didn't kick her out soon, I would have seriously had to hurt her. A few days later, two days after we celebrated the entry of the new year to be exact, I asked her to leave. This brings us to the infamous "eviction" when I put all of Joanne's stuff in the dumpster.

CHAPTER TWENTY-FOUR

The day after I kicked Joanne out, she called my job and told my boss about the elaborate scheme I had used to get hired. After investigating what Joanne told her, I was fired.

At that time Joanne's cousin Sherman, my exboyfriend, was dating this chick named Toya. Although Sherman and I had broken up months before, we never stopped seeing each other. Then after I kicked Joanne out, Sherman and I started spending a great deal of time together.

One day Sherman had come over to my place to visit. He had told Toya some ridiculous story about his whereabouts, but he was actually heading to my place. We were preparing to leave for the movies when his beeper went off.

"Shit. Who is this?" Sherman looked at his beeper and rolled his eyes.

"You know it's Toya. Go ahead and call her back," I said with a slight attitude.

Sherman informed me that it wasn't Toya, it was his mother. "Damn! What does she want?" He called his mother's number back, but was surprised to hear Toya's voice on the other end.

"What's up? Let me speak to my mother."

"Your mother did not beep you, I did," Toya said.

Sherman asked, "For what?" I could tell that he was agitated. He was looking at me out the corner of his eyes, pretending that he was not talking to Toya.

"Where are you?"

"Don't be clocking me. I told you where I was going."

"Whatever, Sherman. I know where you are. You're at Kerri's house, aren't you?" Toya knew something was up.

"I'm a grown ass man. I ain't got to be answering nobody's questions." Sherman was smiling from ear to ear waiting for me to make a scene, but I didn't. I just stood right there and watched him lie like a rug.

He weaseled his way out of that conversation and hung up the phone. Then just before we walked out the door, the telephone rang. I rushed to answer the phone, "Hello."

"Let me speak to Sherman!" Toya must have dialed *69 because Sherman's mother did not have a caller I.D.

"Look, bitch, Sherman don't live here. Don't call my house asking for Sherman no more!" I warned.

I told Sherman to pick up the phone. At first he wouldn't answer, then I grabbed the side of his face and nearly rammed the cordless phone in his ear.

"Alright, Kerri! Damn!" Sherman said as he grabbed the phone. "Hello."

"Sherman, what the fuck is up?" asked Toya.

"Nothing."

"What do you mean nothing? You all up in another bitch face and you telling me aint nothing going on."

"I'm about to roll out. We can talk about this later." Sherman hung up the phone and we went to the movies.

By the time we got back it was after midnight. I kept telling Sherman to go home before he got into more trouble with Toya, but he insisted on staying.

We were preparing for bed when the telephone rang again. "Who the hell is this calling my house this time of night?" I reached over and picked up the phone, "Hello."

"Is Sherman there?" It was Toya.

"Didn't I tell you not to call my house no more?"

"Fuck you! Where is Sherman?" Toya was determined to have the last word.

"He's right here eating my pussy." I knew it was childish to carry on such a conversation with Toya, but I just couldn't resist.

"Bitch, stop lying! Sherman don't even eat pussy."

"That's what you think," I teased.

"Whatever, Kerri. I'm not trippin off that shit you talking. Just tell Sherman to pick up the phone!"

"What is it with you? You don't believe shit stinks, do you?"

"To hell with you, Kerri. I didn't call to talk to you. Let me talk to Sherman!"

"Don't you get it? Sherman does not want your funny looking ass. You're ugly as a pile of shit and your sex is tired. Why would he want an appetizer when he can have the full course meal?" I was hurling insults left and right.

Sherman was undaunted by Toya's persistence. He had told her several times that he didn't like her in the same way that she liked him, but she didn't believe him. As far as Toya was concerned, Sherman was her man whether he liked it or not.

Though I was just trash talking when I said that he was eating my pussy, that gave me an idea.

I continued my childish conversation with Toya and guided Sherman's mouth to the center of my crouch. Gently rubbing the top of his curly head, I could feel his energy as he slowly released spoonfuls of breath while licking my thighs and massaging my clit.

Sherman knew what I liked. He knew that the slightest bump against my insatiable breast would send tantalizing surges from the rounds of my nipples to the tips of my toes. He was a bit of a pussy connoisseur. He knew that the feel of his lips sucking my clit would send shock waves through my body.

His soft, wet lips felt warm on my skin as his tongue created massive waves of pleasure deep inside me. The sensation was incredible. I was so overwhelmed with passion that I started to make sweet noises. The kind of noises that come from an experienced lover's gentle touch. The kind that escapes your lungs when you least expect. The kind that sends chills up and down your spine. "Um, yeah baby, right there." The more Sherman licked, the more noise I made. "That's it, Sherman. Eat this pussy."

I was certain not to hang up the phone. I wanted Toya to hear what she didn't want to hear and to visualize what she didn't want to see. "Don't stop, baby, yes, right there." Just knowing that Toya could hear me made me super horny. "Come on Sherman, eat this pussy." Sherman worked his tongue around the outside of my center, then sucked the membrane located in the northern most part of the vagina. He did it gently, and kissed it with ease. It was driving me crazy, "That's right, Sherman. Suck this pussy." I was so hot. All I wanted was to feel the cool of the rain. "Come on, Sherman, make the rain come down." Not the rain from the sky, but the rain within my body. There was definitely a storm brewing, but I didn't need an umbrella, Sherman's lips would serve that purpose. He knew how to make me feel good.

That went on for a couple of minutes, then my legs started to shake and my knees quivered. My entire body trembled as my inner juices flowed like a raging river. Sweat dripped down my legs as my womanly fluid found its way out. I moaned to let Sherman know the joy he created within. He moaned back. I was in paradise.

Though I was deep into my moment of love with Sherman, I did not forget that Toya was still on the phone. I picked it up and said, "See there, Toya, shit stinks like a motherfucker, don't it?"

Toya pretended that she wasn't listening, as if she was not on the phone, but I heard her breathing. Then her daughter busted her out big time, "Mommy, when are you gonna get off the phone? I'm waiting for you to rock me back to sleep." Just then she hung up.

With the thought of Toya gone, I focused my attention on more important things like allowing Sherman to feast on my womanhood once more.

Sherman treated me to another oral stimulation and I returned the favor. About thirty minutes later I heard someone in front of the apartment building blowing a car horn like there was no tomorrow.

"That better not be who I think it is," I said to Sherman as I peeked out the bedroom window.

"What kind of car is it?" Sherman asked.

"I don't know, it's a little brown car."

"Let me see." Sherman looked out the window. He didn't have to tell me that it was her, his facial contortion and nervous twitch told me all I needed to know. It was Toya alright, and she was directly in front of my apartment blowing her horn like a madwoman at 2:00 in the goddamn morning.

She got out of her car and started to yell, "Sherman! Sherman! I know you hear me, you no good bastard! Come your ass out here!" Toya took turns yelling and blowing the horn.

"Sherman, go out there and talk to her," I demanded.

Despite my insistence, Sherman did not want to deal with Toya. "Fuck her! She better go her ass back home. Ain't nobody trippin' off her." He closed the curtains and walked out into the living room. I followed.

"Sherman! Don't make me come up there and get you! Sherman, bring your black ass outside right now!" Toya was delirious.

I was pissed. Not so much because Toya called herself coming to take Sherman home with her, but because she had the nerve to come to my place of residence with that bullshit. Here it was 2:00 in the morning and this bitch was honking her horn and yelling obscenities like a damn fool. My neighbors were listening, no doubt, and I knew I would hear about it from the rental office in the morning.

"Sherman, you have to go out there and talk to her. She is not gonna leave until you do," I pleaded.

"Baby, don't worry about her. Just go on back to sleep."

"Okay, Sherman. But I'm warning you, if that bitch knocks on my door she's gonna get fucked up." I grabbed a butcher's knife from the cutting block in the kitchen and went back to the bedroom.

"What are you gonna do with that knife?" Sherman asked cautiously.

"Let that bitch knock on my door."

Sherman thought it was a joke. He grinned and asked, "What you gon' do if she knocks on the door?"

"Don't worry about all that. Just let her be bold enough to knock on my goddamn door. Both of y'all will find out."

Toya just wouldn't give up. She had been outside my window blowing her horn, yelling Sherman's name and daring him to come outside for more than thirty minutes. Finally I said to Sherman, "Either you go your ass out there and talk to her or I will."

At that point he started to put on his clothes. He knew that if I had gone out there to talk to Toya somebody was bound to get slapped and it damn sure wasn't going to be me.

I was good at many things, fighting was one of them. And though I did have 75% of the good sense that God gave me, when it came to fighting, that other 25% surfaced. I would zap out and damn near kill a motherfucker before I would let them get the best of me. When I went into battle mode I was five cans short of a six pack, or in other words, I was crazy. I knew it and so did Sherman so he put on his pants and shoes and went outside to talk to Toya.

I told Sherman to say what needed to be said to Toya in a matter of minutes; fifteen to be exact. I looked at my watch and realized that Sherman had been out there talking to Toya for almost an hour. I peeped through the curtains to see what was going on. From what I could tell it was not much. They were standing against Sherman's car talking.

Ten more minutes past, still no sign of Sherman. He was still outside talking to Toya. "That's it! Who the fuck does she think she is?" I said to myself as I started to get dressed.

I essentially went into battle mode. The rear corner of my closet was where I stashed my designated "rumbling gear" which consisted of an old pair of jeans, old Timberland boots and an old rusty jacket. I hadn't disturbed that part of the closet since that whole scene with Joanne a few weeks ago. I got geared up, pulled my long black hair into a bun and asked God to grant me forgiveness if this thing turned into murder.

Though I thought about it for a second, I decided that Vaseline was not needed. There was no way in hell I would let that ugly bitch get anywhere near my beautiful face.

I put the butcher's knife back on the block and took a smaller paring knife instead. If I had to use it, I wanted to be discreet. The size of the butcher's knife would not allow such discretion.

Before I went outside I peeped out the window to see if they were still talking. They were, so I went outside to tell Sherman to either come back inside with me or get his shit

and leave with Toya. One thing was for certain, I would not
sit in the house waiting for him to decide any longer.

When I walked out of the apartment building
Sherman was shocked. "Kerri, go back in the house. I'm
coming, just give me a few more minutes."

I walked over to where they were standing. I didn't
even acknowledge Toya's presence as I said, "You've been
out here long enough, Sherman. Either you come back now
or don't come back ever."

"Kerri, go 'head with that shit. I said I'll be upstairs
in a minute. Just go on back in the house, I'm right behind
you."

"What do you mean you are right behind her? You
just told me that you were coming home with me," Toya
said.

"Oh, he did? That's funny. If my memory serves me
right, I could have sworn I heard him say that he was
through with you, Toya. Ain't that right, Sherman?"

Sherman stood in silence. Both Toya and I were
determined that he was leaving with each of us respectively,
but Sherman didn't know whom he was leaving with. I
knew he really wanted to come back upstairs with me, but
Toya had something on him. After only about three weeks
into their relationship, Sherman had talked Toya into signing
for a fully loaded Lexus GS400 for him to drive.

I didn't know too much about Toya, but signing her
name on the dotted line of a car's bill of sale for a man she
had been dating for only three weeks suggested to me that
she was half crazy, if not completely insane - especially
considering the fact that the financing agreement was for
seventy-two months and the monthly payments on the car
were somewhere in the five to six hundred dollar range.

Any fool could see that Sherman was just using Toya, but she couldn't. She had obviously fallen in love with Sherman and was on the verge of a nervous breakdown when she realized that he did not have the same romantic feelings for her that she had for him.

"Sherman, I'm tired. I am going home. Are you coming or what?" Toya asked. She looked like she had been crying all day and that her eyes would overflow with tears at any moment.

"I'm sorry, Toya, but I'm not going home with you," Sherman said with conceit.

"How come?" Toya aksed.

"Because I am where I wanna be."

CHAPTER TWENTY-FIVE

After the ordeal with Toya, Sherman and I were bona fide boyfriend and girlfriend. We were a couple despite the fact that Joanne had tried to sabotage our relationship.

You see, Sherman and I had been kicking it on the DL for years and nobody knew except Joanne. Then all of a sudden, when Joanne and I fell out, Toya mysteriously found out about me and Sherman's creeping. Even more mysterious, Toya found out where I lived. It doesn't take a rocket scientist to figure that out. Nonetheless, when it was all said and done, Sherman had moved in with me.

Four months later I was in court. Joanne had filed a civil suit against me for illegal eviction and destruction of property. When I received the notice to appear in court and the handwritten complaint she had filed, I was outraged.

Everything she listed as her personal property actually belonged to me. The truth of the matter was that, yes, I did throw her stuff out and, yes, some of her property was destroyed in the process, but that "property" consisted of a few clothing items like shoes, and a tired, cheap ass wrought iron bed. She didn't hardly have several expensive diamond rings, two fur coats, sofa and chair, dining room set, computer, scanner, printer, fax machine and microwave, as she so unlawfully claimed.

In fact, Sherman came to get her T.V. and pictures and, at that point, there was nothing left in my apartment that belonged to her. So where did she get the notion that she had all of these expensive items that I was allegedly holding in my apartment? I'll tell you where, from her everlasting passion to transform herself into me.

Joanne had always envied me and tried her best to copy my fashion and lifestyle. But despite her desire to mimic me, she couldn't figure out how I had gotten as far as I did while she was making practically minimum wage and living just two steps above the poverty line. She was trying to convince the judge that everything in my apartment belonged to her; things that I had scrimped and saved for, things that I had spent my hard earned money on, things that were in my apartment long before she was ever even in the picture.

I had asked my cousins Monica and Melanie to appear in court. I needed someone to back-up my story. The way I saw it, Joanne didn't have any eyewitnesses to attest that I was the one who actually threw her stuff out. For all the court knew, Joanne could have made up that story. She could have come and gotten her things herself and filed a bogus report in retaliation for being asked to leave.

Though I was being sued for several thousand dollars and ownership of my own personal property, I declined the opportunity to retain a lawyer. I had worked with attorneys long enough to understand the judicial system and how it works. First and foremost, as an American Citizen, I'm presumed innocent until proven guilty. Without an admission my guilt would be next to impossible to prove. The only people who witnessed the eviction were Jamillah, Monica and Melanie and you know they weren't about to attest to anything. So I appeared in court prepared for trial.

I sat at the defense table looking almost regal. My perfectly tailored pinstripe suit and black Chanel pumps perpetuated my mien of competence. Though I hadn't been properly trained for such an occasion, I was certain that I would win the case.

Before the commencement of the trial, the judge reminded me of my right to legal representation. He asked if I was sure about my decision to represent myself and I confirmed. At that point the judge stated, "Let the record show that the defendant, Kerri Mitchell, has waived her right to an attorney and has entered herself as counsel in this case before the court." With no further ado, trial was called to session and the first witness was called to testify.

"Do you solemnly swear to tell the truth, the whole truth and nothing but the truth, so help you God?"

"Yes."

"Please state your name before the court."

"Joanne Woodward."

Joanne was dressed in gray drawstring trousers and a plain white blouse. She was answering the prosecutor's questions in a scripted tone, like she had rehearsed each line a thousand times.

When my turn came to cross-examine Joanne, I kept my questions concise and to the point.

"Were you living with me, Kerri Mitchell, the defendant in this case, on or about the date and time as stated in your complaint?" I asked.

"Yes." Joanne's hands were shaking and she looked nervous.

"Were you a lease holder, or in other words, did your name appear in the section marked "Tenant" on the signed lease agreement for the residence at the address listed in your complaint?"

"We had an agreement that-"

"Objection, your honor. The question specifically asked if the witness was listed on the lease agreement. A simple yes or no will do."

I could tell that the judge was impressed with my performance and pleasantly surprised at my pleading skills. His eyebrows formed an arch as he declared, "Sustained. Ms. Woodward, please answer the question yes or no."

Appearing flustered, Joanne took a deep breath then exhaled, "No. My name was not on the lease."

It was all going according to plan. The judge played right into my hand as I wooed him with my arguing technique. I took full advantage of the situation and hammered Joanne with set-up questions.

"Ms. Woodward, in your complaint, you stated that you were illegally evicted by me, Kerri Mitchell, and that I had thrown your clothes in the trash. But in fact, isn't it true that you were never evicted, rather asked to move, and upon agreement to such request, isn't it true that you came to the residence listed in your complaint on the evening in question and personally removed your clothes, shoes, and bed at that time?"

Joanne was stunned. She looked me dead in the eyes and answered, "No! That is not true!"

Joanne's pale face turned a puke-ish shade of red. I had her right where I wanted her. I was setting her up for the kill and she was falling for it. I continued to bombard her with complex questions and meticulously punched devastating holes in her story.

"And, Ms. Woodward, isn't it also true that on the same day and time, your cousin Sherman, along with his mother, came to the same residence and removed your 19 inch color television and two framed pictures or artwork at your request?"

The courtroom was in a frenzy. As I displayed what little skill I had acquired from watching well trained trial attorneys at work and occasional late night Perry Mason reruns, the audience watched in amazement and the judge sat erect with his hand resting firmly on his chin.

No one had expected me to perform so well. After completely contradicting Joanne's claims, I asked three final pivotal questions.

"Ms. Woodward, in your complaint, you stated that several items of your ownership were left in the apartment in which you occupied with me, Kerri Mitchell, the defendant. Can you produce receipts for such items to which you have claimed ownership?"

"No."

"Did you witness me, Kerry Mitchell, the defendant, engage in the alleged illegal eviction or destruction of your personal property?"

"No, I did not."

"Last, but not least, can you produce an eyewitness to any of your claims against me, Kerri Mitchell, the defendant in this case?"

"No."

Joanne looked as if she was about to explode. I, on the other hand, looked poised and professional. Feeling confident that I had dispelled any trace of guilt on my part, I faced the judge and proclaimed, "Your Honor, I have no further questions."

Though Sherman's mother was subpoenaed to appear, I wasn't threatened by her testimony. Sherman was asked to appear as well, but I told him that if he came to court and testified against me he would never get another whiff of this pussy.

Monica and Melanie both corroborated my story. After a damaging cross-examination and fascinating closing argument, the judge had come to a decision.

"I have been a judge in this courtroom for more than twenty years, and I have to say this has been one of the most interesting cases I have ever tried. Ms. Mitchell, I want to congratulate you on a job well done. You might want to go back to school and become a lawyer. As for you, Ms. Woodward, my advice to you is the next time you think about moving in with someone, make sure that you are either a tenant on the lease or have a written agreement between you and the lease holder. Given the lack of evidence submitted before me today, this case is hereby dismissed." And so, with the stroke of his wooden gavel, I avoided restitution and retained my property.

I was so excited that I wanted to jump for joy, but Joanne was not satisfied with the judge's decision. In an effort to try to change the judge's verdict, she pleaded with him to conduct a re-trial. As I was walking through the swinging doors that connected the trial area to the rest of the courtroom, Joanne tried to walk through at the same time.

What I thought was an accidental "bump" into each other, turned into a charge of physical assault as Joanne screamed, "Your Honor, she just bumped me! Did you see that?"

Now I was stunned. Though Monica and Melanie both said that it did look like I had deliberately swung my shoulder at Joanne, I did not do it on purpose. As much as I would have loved to have bumped her on purpose, I would never have done something so stupid.

I pleaded with the judge to listen to me. I was trying to convey to the judge that what had happened was simply an accidental "bump", not my way of making bodily contact with Joanne. I mean think about it, what would have been the point of doing such a thing? I had just put on a fabulous performance before a courtroom full of people and received a judgment in my favor. Why would I have thrown it all away just to get a cheap shot at Joanne? It just didn't make sense. But what, if anything, in my life ever did.

Once again, the courtroom was frenzied. Everybody was talking and trying to figure out what had just happened. Meanwhile, Joanne stood in the corner near the judge, holding her arm as if she was dying from the pain. The judge banged his gavel and warned, "Order in the Court! Order in the Court!"

With a disgusted look and fed-up tone the judge said, "Ms. Mitchell, I saw everything that happened. You deliberately bumped into Ms. Woodward. Now, as far as my decision to dismiss the case against you, that verdict still stands. But on another matter, you willfully displayed disorderly conduct before the court. I am surprised at you. You of all people should have known better than to do such a thing."

"But your Honor, I swear it was an accident," I pleaded.

"Ms. Mitchell, I sat here and watched you bump into Ms. Woodward. Are you calling me a liar?"

"No, Your Honor, I am not calling you anything. I am just telling you that whatever you saw was an accident."

"Ms. Mitchell, I am holding you in contempt of court. I hereby sentence you to five days in jail."

I was so confused, I didn't understand what was going on. The judge sat in his chair gathering his papers as if everything was over and he was preparing to leave.

"But, Your Honor!" I yelled as I tried to get his attention, but he continued thumbing through the papers on his desk. I was furious.

"This is ridiculous. You have got to be kidding me?" I exclaimed.

"Ms. Mitchell, I am ordering you to five days in the county jail whether you like it or not. If you don't be quiet and display some constraint in my courtroom, I'll add five more days to your sentence!"

As the judge stepped down from the stand and entered his chambers behind the courtroom, he instructed the Baliff to handcuff me.

At that point, the courtroom was out of control. Everybody was talking, trying to figure out what was going on. Joanne was standing in the corner with a devilish smirk on her face.

I can remember standing there in my $300 suit and $400 Chanel pumps. I was mad as hell. I stood shackled with handcuffs waiting for someone to jump out and say, "Smile, you're on Candid Camera." I just knew it was all a joke, that the judge was just trying to scare me and that I'd be walking out the door at any moment.

I realized that the judge was serious when the deputy started to log my information in the computer system.

When the paddywagon came to pick me up I thought I was the only one being transported from the courthouse to the jail. I realized that was not the case when I got inside and saw the twenty or so male inmates on the other side of the van. I was the only female in the paddywagon and the only thing that stopped those men from attacking me was a thin wall of bars separating one side of the van from the other.

At first I was quiet. I was still in denial about the entire situation. Then one of the guys asked me what I was "in" for. He commented on how pretty I was and how sexy I looked. He even offered to take me out to dinner as soon as he made parole.

When we arrived at the jail I was dropped off first. I felt like a peace of meat. I had been stripped, searched, poked and fingerprinted. The smell reeked of cigarettes and ammonia. I couldn't wait to get the hell out of there.

I never knew how much I missed my bed until that night. I was in a small holding cell, with a steel toilet that looked like it was on it's last leg, a rusted sink and a flat steel bench that was far too cold to lay down on. Then, I remembered something that an inmate told me the last time I had a run-in with the law. According to this inmate, a roll of toilet paper was a good substitute for a pillow. So I grabbed the toilet paper off the floor, tore off the first few sheets, wet them and threw them at the ceiling for fun, then propped the tissue under my head. It wasn't as comfortable as my pillow at home, but it got me through that first night in jail.

Though I had been arrested two times before that time, I had never stayed a night in jail. With each prior arrest, I was released the same day.

I was awakened by a noise that sounded like the bell that signaled the beginning of first period back in elementary school. It was 4:00 in the morning and I was waiting to hear the sound of squeaky adolescent voices singing "My country 'tis of thee, sweet land of liberty, of thee I sing" when I heard an obnoxious voice say, "Wake up Mitchell. You goin' to pop."

I stretched, yawned, rubbed my tired eyes and asked, "Who is Pop and why am I going to see him?"

The correction officer looked at me like I was crazy. "Pop ain't no person. Pop is jail talk for population. It means you are gettin' your stripes. You goin' in with the rest of them fools, but first you have to change into this." He handed me a plastic bag that contained a bright orange jumper, T-shirt, some dingy white drawers, a pair of dingy white socks, beige shower shoes, blue footies, a wash cloth, towel, bar of soap, teacup, comb, toothbrush and toothpaste. I was officially an inmate.

My first day in jail was actually better than I had expected. The other inmates were extremely friendly and there was more stuff to do there than I had expected. We talked, did each other's hair, played cards, and watched cable T.V. I was excited. I didn't even have cable T.V. at home.

That afternoon we watched music videos, R rated movies and dysfunctional talk shows. I was having more fun in jail than I did on the outside, but after the first few hours, the novelty wore off.

I started to miss my family, especially Hasannah and Randa. Since Hasannah had to go to school, my neighbor agreed to keep her and my mother agreed to keep Randa.

Later that day, about 4:00 in the evening to be exact, dinner was served. While the other inmates were devouring their trays, my food remained untouched. Just looking at the hard bread, mystery meat, cold rice and watery jello made my stomach upset. I sat there turning my nose up at the pitiful excuse for a meal when one of the inmates asked me, "Are you 'gon eat dat?"

"I don't want this shit," I said hastily.

She looked at me, laughed and said, "You'll get used to it."

She obviously didn't know whom she was talking to. I wanted so badly to tell her that, "I am Kerri Mitchell. I am not like you. I won't be getting used to shit. I will be getting the fuck out of here and, when I do, you won't ever see me again," but I didn't. I just looked at her and said, "Whatever."

When phone time came, I had a list of people I wanted to call. First, I tried calling Sherman. He was at my apartment, but I had forgotten about the block I put on my phone when Randall was in the very same jail. Then I tried my mother and she too had a block on her phone. I was so frustrated. Of the six people I tried to call, five of them had blocks on their phones. The only person that didn't have a block on her phone was my grandmother. And though I really didn't want to call her because I didn't want to hear her mouth about what had happened, I was going stir crazy, desperate to engage in a meaningful conversation with a person that was at least half-way intelligent. So I called my grandmother and talked to her for a while.

About ten o'clock that night, the lights were dimmed and we were summoned to our cells. My cellmate or "cellie" as it is commonly known, was new to the jail as well. She was a hefty chick, the equivalent to a female version of Paul Bunyun. She didn't say much to me and I hardly acknowledged her presence, until she decided that she had privilege to the top bunk.

I had already placed my plastic bag full of jail necessities at the foot of the top bunk, but she decided that particular section of the bunk belonged to her. With a swift one-handed move, she flung my bag down on the floor.

I was pissed. I thought to myself *How dare she move my bag like she's running things?* I said, "Excuse me! What do you think you are doing?"

She answered, "I was just moving your bag. It was on my bed."

She slid onto the upper bunk, lay down with her hands under her head and gave me a look that said fuck you and your bag. As if that wasn't enough, she had the nerve to say, "What's up with those cookies...you gonna eat 'em?"

I stood there trying my best not to grab her neck and squeeze every inch of breath from her lungs. I thought to myself *I don't believe this bitch.* She had more nerve than a little bit. First she had the audacity to move my things without asking me. Then she had the balls to ask for one of the cookies I had saved from the slop that was masquerading as my dinner. Right away, I knew she had the game fucked up. I'd seen her kind before. Since she was the size of not one, but two elephants, she thought she could chump me, but I had news for her. She might have been huge, and she might have had a twisted view of my boxing efficiency, but I wasn't having it. I didn't care how twisted her view of me was, I was pissed off at her belligerence and was prepared to straighten any confusion out for her.

I nicely grabbed my bag, pushed her legs to the side and put my bag right back where it was.

She just got up and climbed down to the bottom bunk. Just as I was about to lay down she said, "So what's up, you gonna give me one of those cookies or what?"

I sat on the edge of my bunk and replied, "Not even if my life depended on it."

The next morning I was awaken by the searing bell and the sound of the cell blocks unlocking. It was time to rise and shine.

After breakfast we just sat around and did not do much of anything. I was so ready to go home. I had been there for two nights and to make matters worse, it was Friday.

Jail is the last place on earth I wanted to be, especially for something as petty as bumping into someone. But there was no need to bitch and complain, I had been sentenced to five days and had three more days left to serve.

Later that day, after the mail was distributed, we were having dinner. It was around 4:00 in the evening. One of the inmates was excited because she was to be released that day. We were sitting at the table chatting when an officer walked into our unit.

"Aww shit….somebody's about to get out of here." Said one of the inmates.

"Let me get my things, he's coming for me," said the lady who was waiting to be released.

As everyone was getting excited to see who was leaving, I got depressed. I knew I had at least three more days to go so I wasn't excited about anything.

The officer walked up to the door and yelled, "Okay ladies, I have a list of names to be released today. If you hear your name, get your shit and follow me."

The officer rambled off four names before he said, "Kerri Mitchell."

When I heard my name I was surprised. I thought he had called the wrong person so I just sat there. Then he said it again. At that point I realized that the judge must have changed his mind and ordered my release so I jumped up and ran to the front of the short line of inmates.

Just before we left, my cellmate came running over to me, yelling, "Kerri, you forgot your bag."

I turned around and said, "Thanks, but no thanks. I no longer need it."

The first person I saw when I walked out of the jail was Sherman. He was so happy to see me.

He told me that my mother had been calling the jail everyday asking for my release. I didn't know what I had done to make the judge change his mind, but obviously he had a change of heart because I was no longer in prison.

When I got home I went to pick up the kids and called everyone to let them know that I was home again.

The two nights I spent in jail were an eye opener. I had time to think about everything that went on. As a result of my ignorance to a so-called friend's ulterior motives, I had once again been the lead character in an episode of extreme drama.

You would think that I'd had enough. But as the months went by, I proved that I had an insatiable attraction to extreme drama and the chaos that ultimately followed.

CHAPTER TWENTY - SIX

It was now the beginning of summer and I had moved to a cute little rambler in the same town a few miles away.

After receiving notice that my apartment was going up on the rent, I decided to rent a house instead. Sherman moved in with me and before long, we were arguing everyday.

Since he wasn't working, he would babysit for me while I worked. I would get the girls dressed and comb their hair in the morning so that all Sherman would have to do was keep an eye on them. I was hoping that maybe he would take them outside to play or to see a movie occasionally. But Sherman was lazy. Most of the time he would have the girls sitting in the house all day and would be just waking up when I was about to get off from work.

Though Sherman didn't work, he did a little something on the side and provided me with a couple of hundred dollars every week. In the beginning I didn't ask him to pay any bills because he was always giving me money. But when $200 turned into $100 and sometimes as little as $50 a week, I started charging him rent.

He claimed he didn't mind paying rent, but when that time of the month rolled around, Sherman would have every excuse in the world as to why he couldn't pay me right then and there. His favorite line was, "I'll pay you on Friday," but when Friday came he would promise to pay on Sunday. Then Sunday turned into Tuesday or Wednesday and before I knew it, it was Friday again and I still didn't have the money he had promised to pay on the previous Friday.

Sherman was going through hard times. He would make all kinds of promises that he couldn't keep. He owed everybody and their momma money, including his own. This was new for me. I had never dealt with a man who didn't have any money. In fact, I would never give them a chance. But there was something different about Sherman. Even though he was seemingly broke, he pretended very well. But soon I started to see through the masquerade and slowly but surely our relationship started to deteriorate.

It started with Sherman's Lexus. It had started to fall apart. Though his car was in dire need of repair, he was still driving it. He didn't have any insurance and had missed several finance payments. But he wasn't worried about the car being repossessed by the snatch man because he knew that the financing company didn't know where the car was.

I tried talking him into turning the car in, but he wouldn't listen. I couldn't understand why he even wanted to keep it. He couldn't afford it. Not only was he behind in the monthly payments, he couldn't afford the daily maintenance. It was falling apart piece by piece and, since Sherman didn't have any money, there was nothing he could do about it. The air-conditioning, power windows, and gas gauge were all on the blink. He had gotten into an accident and had a big dent and chipped paint on the driver's side.

Sherman was ridiculous. It would be 100 degrees outside and he would be profiling in that hot ass car! I mean the leather seats would be so hot that you could fry bacon on the back of his thighs. The air-conditioning was spurting hot air, the driver's side window wouldn't roll down, and the passenger side window was rolled all the way down and wouldn't roll back up. There could have been a tank full of gas in the car, but the gauge was stuck on "E" so he was constantly stopping at the gas station putting in five dollars here, ten dollars there to make sure that it wasn't empty. You couldn't listen to music because the speakers were busted and there was a tape stuck in the cassette. And to make matters worse, he had the car for about six months and was still driving around with temporary tags . . . and they weren't even legit! He had gotten pulled over by the police so many times due to the counterfeit tags that I let him use some tags I had from a previous car.

A few months past and Sherman still wasn't making any progress. I told myself that if he didn't get his shit together soon, it would be curtains for him.

I had dealt with his financial issues as long as I could stand and finally told him to leave, but he thought it was a joke. He told me he wasn't going anywhere and that I had better stop playing with him.

I didn't realize it at the time, but Sherman was crazy. He had been putting on an act for as long as I knew him. Before he moved in, I only saw his good side. But after we were living together, I recognized just how simple he was.

One day I had went with him to visit his mother. We went inside and left his car parked directly in front of his mother's house. We were sitting in the kitchen when Sherman's mother came running inside. She was breathing like she had just run a marathon. "Sherman, come here quickly!"

"What's up, Mamma?" Sherman asked.

"Wasn't that your Lexus parked in front of the house?"

"Yeah, why?" Sherman got up and started walking towards the front door. He opened the door and didn't see his car, "Shit! The snatch man must'a got that joint!"

"The snatch man? What damn snatch man?" Sherman's mother was standing in the doorway trying her best to contain her laughter.

"Damn! I knew I shouldn't have parked my whip around here!"

At that point, she couldn't hold back the laughter any longer. She was cracking up. She shook her head and said, "Boy. . .ain't no damn snatch man got your car. . .I just saw Toya get in your car and drive off down the street."

"Toya?" Sherman was puzzled.

"I'm telling you boy, that was Toya." Sherman's mother got a kick out of it. She had been trying to convince him to turn the car in as well.

"Why didn't you stop that bitch? Why would you just sit there and watch her take my shit like it's hers?" Sherman was pissed.

Then I butted in the conversation, "Because it is hers!"

Sherman shot me a damning look and yelled, "Why don't you mind your own damn business?"

"You are my business, therefore I am minding my own business! I told your stupid ass to turn the car in. That car is still in Toya's name and you haven't made a payment in months. Did you think she was just going to sit around and let you keep driving it?"

"Man, fuck that shit you talking, Kerri. Ain't nobody trynna hear that! I'm about to go and get my whip from that bitch! And when I catch her I'mma bust her in her fuckin' mouth!"

That's when Sherman's mother got serious. "Look here Sherman, don't bring all that raucous up in my house! You ain't got nobody to blame but yourself! If I've told you once, I've told you a thousand times, you can't go 'round doin' people dirty. Toya had every right to take that car back. You can't be fucking up people's credit! She should have never gotten the car in her name . . . and furthermore, she should have never fucked with you in the first place."

Sherman didn't say anything. He just stood in the doorway with his hands resting in his empty pockets and his head hung low.

"I don't know why you standing over there looking like Sad Sammy, you should've expected this to happen. Shit, Sherman, y'all ain't even together anymore!" Sherman knew his mother had a point, but he did not want to admit it. He insisted on finding Toya and reclaiming his car.

Weeks past and Sherman had given up on getting the Lexus back. Though I was glad that Toya did take the car, I was beefing because she refused to return my tags.

Then one day while visiting a friend in nearby
Clinton, Maryland, I spotted Sherman's Lexus on a
residential street. It still had that big dent on the driver's
side and there was a giant plastic trash bag covering the
passenger side window.

I pulled over on the side of the road. "Kerri, what are
you doing?" asked my friend Jenny. She was riding shotgun.

"That's Sherman's Lexus. I'm about to get my tags
back."

"How do you know it's Sherman's Lexus?" Jenny
asked.

"Because I know his car and I know my tags, duh!" I
hissed.

"What if somebody sees you?" Jenny was scared.

"I don't give a damn who sees, those are my tags and
I'm about to take what belongs to me!" I was as serious as a
heart attack. I grabbed a screwdriver from under my seat,
walked over to Sherman's Lexus and reclaimed my property.
Jenny's scared ass waited for me in my car.

Now that Sherman didn't have a ride, our
relationship was really strained. He was still watching the
kids for me and I would let him keep my car while I was at
work.

I didn't ask much of Sherman, just that he watch the
kids and keep his trifling friends out of my place when I was
not at home. In fact, his friends were banned from my house
even when I was home.

They were the saddest bunch of so-called men I've
ever seen. They were all in their mid to late twenties, most
of them didn't have jobs, girlfriends nor cars. Only one of
them had a ride, but he lived at home with his mamma like
the rest of them.

I didn't give them a chance to latch onto me. I saw how they took advantage of Sherman's mother. After witnessing Sherman's best friend Reggie connive his way into shacking up on Sherman's mother's living room sofa, I knew I had to feed his friends with ten-foot spoons.

Sherman and I would get into heated arguments over my disapproval of his friends. He would tell me that I was too judgmental and that if I would take the time to get to know his friends, I would like them. But I had no intentions of getting to know them and couldn't have cared less whether they liked me or not. I gave Sherman strict instructions to keep his friends out of my house. As far as I knew, he upheld that standard. But then, one day after catching him in a lie, he confessed that he had been having company while I was at work.

He had called me at work to chat and I heard someone talking in the background. "Who is that, Sherman? I know you don't have none of those trifling ass friends of yours in my house?"

"Nah, ain't nobody in here with me. That's just the T.V." he assured me.

Then I heard someone laugh. "Sherman, who the fuck is that?" I was pissed. He was trying to convince me that there was no one in the house with him.

Later that evening when I got home, Sherman was sitting in the living room chair with his feet rested on the matching ottoman. He had been home all day and the house was a mess. There were video games and VHS movies scattered across the living room floor. The cushions from the couch were scattered about and the kitchen floor was sticky from the soda he had wasted. There were popcorn kernels on the carpet and all kinds of junk between the couch cushions. Though he tried to cover up the smell with strawberry scented Glade air freshener, the poignant scent of freshly burned marijuana leaves overpowered me as soon as I walked through the door.

"Sherman! What the hell happened in here? Why is this house so filthy?" He didn't answer. "Sherman! Do you hear me talking to you? What happened in here today?"

"Nothing." He rolled his eyes as he answered. "I was just about to start cleaning up. I didn't expect you to be home so early."

"It looks like you had a fuckin' party in here!"

"Ain't nobody have no damn party. I've been in here by myself all day, chillin."

"Chillin, huh?"

"Yeah, chillin.'"

I was pissed. I stepped over the mounds of trash and walked into the kitchen. My eyes went straight to the sink.

"Sherman, did you have your trifling ass friends over here today?"

"No."

"Just tell the truth, Sherman. Did you have company?"

"Nah, I told you, I've been here by myself all day. Besides, I know the rules, my friends are not welcome here."

"Are you sure about that?"

"Yes, I'm sure."

"Well, why are there three cups, three bowls and three fuckin' spoons in my kitchen sink?" Sherman was busted.

"Damn, Kerri! Who are you, Perry fuckin' Mason?"

"Whatever. This isn't about me. This is about you disregarding the house rules."

"Whatever Kerri," Sherman said as he stretched and yawned. Then I noticed a shiny silver handle tucked inside Sherman's pants. "Sherman, what is that in your pants? It better not be what I think it is."

"Goddamn! Go 'head with that shit, Kerri!"

"How many times do I have to tell you not to bring guns in here? You know how I feel about guns!"

"Kerri, you know a nigga gotta stay strapped. You never know what kinda drama might kick off. I just wanna be prepared if something goes down."

"Well, when you get your own place you can stay strapped all you want, but right now you are living with me and my two kids, therefore, keep your strap outta my house!"

I walked over to the coffee table and picked up an empty box of Phillies Blunts. "What is this? Didn't I tell you not to smoke in my house?"

"Your house? Why you keep talking about your house?"

"Yes, motherfucker, my house . . . and no friends, no guns and no smokes are my rules!"

"Fuck you and your rules! I'm tired of hearing about your rules. In case you haven't noticed, I'm a grown ass man!"

I threw the empty box of blunts in his lap. "Yeah, you a grown man alright. Sitting around watching stupid ass movies, smoking weed all day, staying strapped. Yeah, Sherman, you a real fuckin' man." I shook my head and mumbled, "A man, huh? Whatever. I can't tell."

"What's that you say? You can't tell? You sure
don't be talking all that trash when I'm fucking the shit out
of you. You can tell then, can't you?"

"Nigga please! You swear you're Superman in the
bedroom!" I chuckled and teased. "Superman my ass! Here
lately you've been more like Boy Wonder!"

Sherman jumped up and walked over to me. With
his index finger about ¾ of inch away from my forehead he
balled up his fist and yelled, "I'm tired of your shit, Kerri!
I'm sick of you telling me what I can and can not do, who I
can and can not have over. You ain't the only person that
lives here, this is my house too!"

"Nigga fuck you! This is my shit! You don't pay no
bills around here!" I stormed off to the living room.

"Oh, so now it's fuck me . . . I don't pay no bills
around here. Who the fuck you think helped you get in this
damn house?"

"So what you gave me the money for the security
deposit! You haven't done shit else since we've been living
here. All the fuck you do is lay around, smoke weed all day,
and watch stupid ass movies!"

Sherman followed me to the living and jumped in my
face again. "So now I don't do shit?"

"Right. You don't do shit but get on my
motherfuckin' nerves!" I pushed his hand out of my face
and walked back to the kitchen.

Sherman followed behind me ranting and raving. "I
watch your kids for you, but I guess that's not good enough.
I guess you need a nigga with some cheese so you can spend
that shit up, huh? That's what you need, right?"

"No. What I need is for you to start helping me out
around here."

"I do help you out. What other nigga you know gonna watch your kids for you?"

"Shit, Sherman. You act like you are supposed to get a medal for that. It's the least you can do. You ain't paying no bills, you don't give me no money, hell, the sex ain't even all that no more. I'm starting to wonder what I need you for."

"So what are you saying?"

"I'm just saying that I need to re-evaluate our relationship."

Sherman reached into his pocket and pulled out a half- smoked joint. He lit his marijuana cigarette from the flame that was burning on the stove, took one extra long drag, then extinguished the smoke by pressing it on the countertop.

He stared me up and down, waiting for me to say something about what he had just done, but I didn't. Then, he let out a boisterous scream of rage and punched a whole the size of China in the kitchen wall.

Still waiting for me to react to his childish tantrum, I gave him a pitiful look and said, "You need Jesus," then I turned the kitchen light out and left him standing there in the darkness. He followed behind me.

"Where are you going?" Sherman asked.

"Outta here, yo' ass is trippin'!" I was determined to get away from him.

"Well, goodbye then! Get the hell on!"

"Oh, don't worry, I will. And I when I return your trifling ass better be gone!" I grabbed my purse and walked out the door.

Three hours later I returned and Sherman was still there. He was watching T.V. as if nothing had happened. I walked into the den and asked, "Why are you still here?"

He kept watching T.V. as if I wasn't standing there. Then I walked over to the entertainment center and stood in front of the T.V.

"Move, Kerri! I can't see the T.V.!"

"So I guess this stupid ass T.V. show is more important than what I'm talking about?"

He rolled his eyes and said, "Just move out of my way!" That's when I turned the T.V. off.

"What the fuck are you doing? I was watching that!"

"C'mon, Sherman, get your shit and go!"

"So you really want me to leave, huh?" Sherman looked so pitiful.

"Yes, I want you outta my house."

He got up, went into the bedroom and started to pack his things.

I tried my best to ignore him and let him leave peacefully, but he was determined to make a scene. He walked over to me with his duffle bag on his shoulder. "So you ain't gonna try and stop me?"

"For what? I said what I had to say."

He tried his best to patch things up. "Are you sure about this?" he asked.

"Yes, I'm sure."

Sherman just wouldn't give up. "So you really want me to leave?"

"Yes, Sherman! Get the fuck out!"

"Alright Kerri, but I'm warning you. If I walk out that door, I'm not coming back."

"Bye! Shit! Get the fuck on!" I wanted him out of my house.

Sherman was relentless. He walked over to me and asked, "So, you really mean this?"

"What part of 'get the fuck out' don't you understand?"

Sherman threw his hands up in the air and yelled, "Bitches! Can't live with them, can't live without them," then he grabbed his duffle bag full of socks, drawers and CDs and headed for the door.

"I know you ain't just call me no bitch?"

"Like I said, bitches! Y'all always complaining about y'all ain't got no man, then when you get one, you treat 'em like shit. All you bitches the same, ain't never satisfied!"

"Well maybe if y'all so-called men would stop being so damn trifling, a bitch would be satisfied!"

Sherman put his duffle bag down and walked over to where I was sitting. He sat down next to me and tried to put his arms around me. "Okay, baby, I'm sorry. Maybe you're right. I'll try harder to please you."

"Get off of me, Sherman!" I got up and moved to the other side of the den. Then he came over and tried to hug me again.

"Stop it, Sherman! Don't touch me!"

"Okay, okay. If that's how you wanna act, fine. I won't touch you."

"Good! Now get your stuff and get out of my house before I call the police!"

"But Kerri, you know I don't have nowhere else to go."

"That sounds like a personal problem to me."

Sherman put his head in his hands, sat down on the couch and mumbled, "I can't believe this bitch is trynna carry me like a sucker."

I told Sherman that I was going in the bedroom to lay down and that when I woke up I expected him to be gone. When I woke up Sherman was still sitting on the couch with his hands in his head and his duffle bag on the floor next to him.

"Sherman, why are you still here?"

"Reggie was supposed to come and pick me up. I don't know what's taking him so long."

"Well I wish he would hurry up! I want you out of my house!"

"Can you at least give me a ride then?"

"Are you crazy?"

"Why are you treating me like this? I ain't never did nothing to you. All I ever did was try to help you, Kerri. But I see now, you are all for yourself."

He kept looking at his watch, then he asked to see the phone so that he could call a cab.

About fifteen minutes later the cab was in the driveway. Sherman just sat there in a daze.

"Okay, Sherman. Your cab is here."

"You might as well tell that cab to go on about his business, Kerri. I told you I don't have nowhere else to go."

"Yes, you do. Go to your mother's house."

"There's not enough room. You know Reggie is staying over there."

"Reggie is your friend, not your brother. Why can't he stay with his own mother? Why does he have to stay at your mother's house?"

"His mother doesn't want him in her house."

"Well, good for her. I don't blame her."

"C'mon now, Kerri. You know I don't have any place to go."

"Just tell your mother to let you stay there. I'm sure she'll understand."

Sherman sat down beside me and put his arm around my neck. The cab driver was steadily honking his horn and Sherman was trying his best to win my sympathy.

"Can I just stay here until I get myself together?"

"Hell no! You should have been had your shit together!"

"C'mon Kerri, please? I swear I'mma start looking for a job tomorrow."

"Sherman, you've been talking that same shit for the past six months."

"I promise, baby. Please, just give me one more chance. I promise I'mma get myself together."

"I'm sorry Sherman. I can't continue to live like this."

"Please, Kerri. Please, don't leave me. You're all I have."

I looked at my watch and said, "Times a wasting and your cab is waiting."

"Please, Kerri. Don't do this to us."

I stood up and pointed towards the front door. "Goodbye, Sherman. I wish you well."

Sherman stood there with tears running down his face. "Please, Kerri. Don't do this."

He was pissing me off so bad. He thought his little helpless in distress act was going to move me to the point of letting him stay, but I could not be swayed. "Sherman, I want you out of my house." I took his hand and guided him to the front door.

"Kerri, please don't do this. I love you."

Before closing the door, I looked him dead in the eyes, gave him a kiss on the cheek and said, "I love you too, but love can't pay my bills."

CHAPTER TWENTY · SEVEN

Sherman had been gone for about a month. In that time he had found a job as a construction worker. Since he was working and trying to better himself I decided to give him another chance.

We'd only been back together for a few weeks when I received a call from Jamillah. She told me that she had run into Randall earlier that day and that he had asked about me.

"Girl, fuck Randall. I haven't seen his trifling ass in almost a year. He hasn't sent any money for the kids or so much as called to say hello. The next time you see Randall, tell that bastard I said he can kiss my entire black ass!"

Later on that night, I had just washed and wrapped my hair and was getting ready to sit under the hooded dryer, when I saw high beam headlights flashing in my driveway.

Who the hell is that coming over here this time of morning? I thought to myself. I rushed to the front door and peeked out the window. It was so dark outside that I couldn't tell what kind of car it was, so I turned on the porch light.

The shinny black SUV sparkled in the glow of the moonlight as I caught a glimpse of the fresh red and white paper tags. I thought it must have been someone coming for Sherman because I didn't know anyone who drove a Lincoln Navigator.

Then, just as I was about to wake Sherman, the doorbell rang. I looked out the peephole, but it was so dark outside that I couldn't tell whom it was.

"Who is it?" I asked cautiously.

"Open up and see."

I knew that voice, but it didn't make any sense. I couldn't figure out why Randall was ringing my doorbell at damn near 1:00 in the morning.

"What do you want?" I asked.

"I need to talk to you," he said.

I cracked the door open just far enough to see Randall's glassy eyes and smell his drunken breath.

"Okay, Randall, you have five minutes. Start talking."

"Can I come in?"

"No, you can not come in. Whatever you need to say can be said right here."

I stood in the doorway and listened to Randall go on and on about a bunch of nothing.

"Okay, Randall. Your five minutes are up."

"Wwwait a minute, Kerri. Let me come in and ttttalk to you. I have a lot of stuff on my mind and I just wanna tttalk to you."

"Now is not a good time. Maybe we can hook up tomorrow and go somewhere and talk."

"Nnnow is the ppperfect tttime!" Randall was so drunk that his words slurred as they found their way out of the crack of his mouth.

"Yeah, maybe for you it is, but not for me. I have company."

"Cccompany?"

"Yes, Randall. I have company. Why don't you go home and get some rest? Give me a call tomorrow and we can talk, okay?"

Randall lifted his bottle of liquor up to his face and started talking to the bottle as if it could understand what he was saying. "Hey RRRemy, yyyou hear that shshit? Aaain't this a bbbitch? I'm ssstanding here 1:00 in the morning pppouring my hhheart out to my whoring ass wwwife and she tttellin' me that nnnow is not the rrright time 'cause she has cccompany!"

"That's enough, Randall. I think you need to leave."

"Nnno! I think yyyou need to tell that bbbitch ass nnnigga you got laying up in there to lllleave!"

"Why do you think you can just pop up over here making demands? I haven't heard from your ass in a whole fucking year! You have no right to come over starting shit on my property!" Randall tried to barge his way in but I pushed him back.

"Wwwhere my kkkids at?"

"You haven't been worrying about your kids, why are you so worried about them now?"

"Yyyou bbbetter not have that nnnigga nowhere near my kkkids!"

"Randall, please go home! You are drunk!"

"I'm not dddrunk!"

"You are so drunk you can't even speak right!"

"I mmmight can't ssspeak right, bbbut I bet I'll bust a cccap in that nnnigga's aaass if he goes anywhere near my ffffuckin' kkkids!"

"Okay, Randall. I really think you need to leave."

"I ain't gggoing nowhere 'til I see my kkkids."

Randall was barely standing up straight.

"So now it's all about the kids, huh?"

"KKKerri, lllet me in! I wanna see my kkkids!"

"Get away from my door, Randall, before I call the police!"

"Ffffuck the police! You better tell that bbbitch ass nigga to get the ffffuck out! I wanna talk to my wife and kkkids!"

"I'm warning you, Randall, get away from my house with that bullshit!"

"Lllet me in, dddammit!" His words slurred as he staggered closer to me. "I'm your mmmotherfuckin' husband! You *my* wwwife! Dem *my* kkkids! Y'all *my* ffffamily! That bbbitch ass nigga better get his down damn ffffamily!"

Randall was making so much noise that I just knew he was going to wake Sherman up. Then, just as I was about to shut the door, he barged his way in and nearly knocked me down in the process.

"What the fuck do you think you are doing?" I yelled as he frantically paced back and forth across the living room floor.

"Aight, KKKerri. I'mma give you tttwo minutes to get that bbbitch ass nigga outta here! After that, I'mma rrrun his ass outta here myself!"

"Randall, what is wrong with you?"

"Yyyou got one minute llleft, KKKerri."

I ran to the kitchen and grabbed the phone. "I'mma call the police if you don't get out of my house!"

"Fffuck the police!"

Now I knew I was in trouble. Randall was drunk as a skunk and didn't have a care in the world. He was threatening to go in my bedroom and kick Sherman's ass if I didn't go in there and tell him to get out.

I tried to talk some since into Randall, but it didn't work. He snatched the telephone off the wall and headed for my bedroom.

"Randall, no! Please leave!"

"Fffuck this shit, KKKerri. You my wwwife, that nigga gotta go!"

Randall barged in my bedroom and turned on the light, "Wwwake the fffuck up, bbbitch ass nigga!" He was standing over Sherman yelling every name he could dredge up. "Ggget the fffuck up! That's my bbbed you lllaying on! Ggget the fffuck out!"

I couldn't believe my eyes and ears. I ran over to Randall and started pushing him out of my bedroom.

I don't know where I got the strength from, but I pushed and pulled Randall's drunk ass all the way from my bedroom to the front door.

Ironically, my mother was staying at my house that night. She heard all the commotion so she got up and ran out into living room.

"Kerri, what the hell is going on?" She thought that Sherman and I were fighting. Then she realized that it was Randall, not Sherman.

"Randall? Is that you?" My mother was baffled.

"Hhhey MMMa, tell KKKerri to get that bbbitch ass nigga outta here!" Randall was so inebriated that he struggled to free his words.

My mother got in front of Randall and pulled his shirt while I stood behind him and pushed as hard as I could. We pushed and pulled his intoxicated body until he was finally out the front door. I hurried and slammed the door before Randall could get back inside.

Randall didn't leave right away. He stood on the porch and performed for about ten minutes or so. When he realized that I wasn't going to open the door, he got in his shinny new Navigator and rolled out.

As soon as Randall's truck disappeared from the driveway Sherman came out of the bedroom with fire in his eyes. "Man, that's some fucked up shit, Kerri!"

"Sherman, baby, I'm sorry. I'm so sorry. I didn't know-"

Sherman interrupted me. "How you gon' let that nigga come up in here raising hell?"

"I'm sorry, Sherman. I tried to keep him out of my bedroom!"

"What? Why did you open the door in the first fuckin' place?"

"I don't know. He said he just wanted to talk. I didn't think he was gonna barge his way in like that."

"Man, that's fucked up! I don't believe you let that shit happen! That nigga could have killed me! I'm laying up here like it's all good! All vulnerable and shit! And you gon' let that drunk ass nigga come rollin' up in here pulling my card like that!"

"I'm sorry, Sherman. I tried to stop him."

Sherman was pissed. He kept peeking out the window to see if Randall came back. "Now you see why a nigga need to have a gun on him? This nigga barging up in your bedroom and I ain't got gun the first! He could have blasted my ass!"

I felt so bad. Sherman was delirious. He started flicking off. "Man fuck this! Who the fuck that nigga think he is? He must think I'mma lil' bitch or something! Fuck that! I'll show his punk ass!"

Sherman put on his clothes and went into the bedroom to use the telephone. I don't know who he was talking to, but whoever it was listened to Sherman rant and rave about what had just happened and how he needed to come and get the "Nine", the "Ooh-whop" and the "AK".

Sherman pranced around the house raising hell for what seemed like hours. Then finally, a car full of his friends pulled up and Sherman rolled out.

A few weeks went past before Sherman spoke to me again. He was still mad at me for letting Randall run up on him like that.

For a while I didn't see Sherman. He knew how I felt about guns and since I would not allow him to bring guns in my house he refused to visit. That incident with Randall had scared him something terrible and he vowed to never step foot in my house again unless he was strapped, so I started to spend more time visiting Sherman at his mother's house.

A few months had past and Randall had started to come around more often. He would call almost everyday to check on the girls and even started to make regular child support payments. We made plans to file for divorce and vowed to remain civil.

Sherman was back to his old self. He got fired from his construction job and was still smoking, carrying guns and hanging with his no-good friends. He still didn't have his own car and his mother had kicked him out because the two of them couldn't get along.

CHAPTER TWENTY - EIGHT

"Sherman, we need to talk." That was the last thing I remembered before the lights in my head went out.

By the time I recovered from the paralyzing blows to my skull, I felt the warmth of my fresh blood trickle down the sides of my face. The 27-inch T.V. felt like a ton of bricks on my back as I lay paralyzed from the neck down.

"Help. Somebody, help me." I screamed in silence. "Help me. Somebody, anybody." I tried with all of my might to yell, but the only thing that came out of my mouth was a soft whisper. Then I started to talk to God, "Please, don't let me die." I tried my best to move, but my entire body was frozen. "Lord, please, don't let me die, I'm not ready to die." I lay there motionless, crying, praying, waiting for someone to rescue me.

I didn't know what had happened. I knew I had
planned on leaving Sherman for good and that there would
be no more second chances for him. I had planned to tell
Sherman to leave my house, but the last thing I remembered
was telling Sherman that I needed to talk to him. The next
thing I knew, I was on the floor with a pool of blood
surrounding my head and a 27inch television was on my
back.

By the time the police arrived I had slipped into a
state of unconsciousness.

I couldn't move nor make any noise, but I heard
everything the police said. I heard them talking from the
moment they opened the door. "Hey, Sergeant, come here.
You gotta see this."

"What tha'-"

"Looks like somebody set a bomb off in here," one of
the officers said.

"No bomb, just a few cinder blocks," said another.

"Goddamn! Whoever did this must have had help.
There's no way one person could do all of this damage
alone."

Sherman had thrown enormous, cement cinder blocks
through each and every window in the house, which left
glass scattered all over the floor. My car sat in the driveway
with all four tires slit, and the windows were busted.

"Hey, Sergeant . . . you ain't gonna believe this."

The voices were getting closer to me. Just then one
of the officers said, "Back here! Come, quickly! There's a
lady and she's beat up pretty badly. Looks like she was
pistol whipped."

"Come on, guys, let's get her some help," the officer
said as he knelt down beside me.

"Hurry! Quick, call an ambulance!"

CHAPTER TWENTY · NINE

That was twenty pounds and fifteen years ago. I'm now 40-years-old and my life couldn't be better. Though physically I recovered, it took me years of therapy to recover emotionally.

After Sherman beat me up and destroyed all of my worldly possessions, I went through months of physical therapy to regain my motor skills.

Luckily I survived. The doctors said I had lost so much blood that if the police hadn't arrived when they did, I probably would not have pulled through.

After that incident, Sherman tried to skip town. He and Reggie had stolen a car and were planning to make a run for it. The very next day they were stopped by a police officer for a routine traffic violation. They both had warrants for their arrest so they tried to get away, but it didn't work. The police chased them down and Sherman ended up spending ten years in jail for a variety of charges

including vehicle theft, destruction of property and
attempted murder.

Ironically, on the day of our divorce hearing, Randall
did not show up. He had taken the wheel while drunk for the
last time. His Navigator was found just two blocks away
from divorce court. An almost empty bottle of Remy Martin
was nestled in the armrest and the signed divorce papers lay
in an envelope on the passenger's seat. Randall's drunken
body lay dead from a head-on collision.

Though I haven't seen Joanne since the day of the
trial, she moved to the west coast and is reportedly the
mistress of a famous actor, or so I've heard.

After that last mental breakdown, my mother started
therapy and taking medication regularly. I'm pleased to say
that she is in great health and our relationship is stronger
than ever.

Hasannah and Randa are both grown with families of
their own. Randa moved to California and is pursuing a
career in acting. She married a successful businessman and
just gave birth to my first grandchild.

Hasannah graduated from law school with honors
and is considered one of the top litigators on the east coast.
She is scheduled to marry her college sweetheart next June.

It might have taken me a while, but I finally got it.
After years of chasing men and money, I learned to chase my
dreams instead. I always knew I had it in me to do good
things.

When I received the money from Randall's life
insurance policy I went back to school and graduated with a
degree in psychology. I knew I wanted to work with abused
women in my old neighborhood of Southeast D.C., but there

weren't any programs that fit that description, so I opened the first shelter for battered and abused women east of the Anacostia River.

I renovated an abandoned building on Martin Luther King Avenue and, in no time, realized my life's mission.

I bring a unique quality to the women at my shelter. Unlike other counselors, I used to be them, not some rich lady who feels sorry for them nor someone who just needs to complete a few hours of community service to keep the judge off her back. I am an abused single mother who grew up in the inner city.

By the time these women find their way into my shelter they have exhausted every other option. They don't want to be around people who make them feel worse, they want to be surrounded by women who know what they are feeling; women who have been there and done that. That's where I step in.

They need an example to show them that they too can make it and that's exactly what I strive to do.

Often times, these women don't come alone, they have their children with them.

I know how it feels to raise innocent children without a male figure. I know how it feels to get your lights punched out by a man who claims to love you. I know how it feels to be called dirty names. And I know how hard it is to walk away. I understand their pain so I am there to give them love and to offer my support. My motto is "You may have been through hell and back, but you don't have to go there anymore."

I'm often asked if I had my life to do over again, what would I change? I can honestly say, "Not a damn thing."

I thank God for the Randalls, Shermans and Joannes of the world. I thank God for each and every miserable person I have ever come across, for if it weren't for their lessons in misery, I wouldn't know the joy I know now. I wouldn't know the mercy of God and I wouldn't know the power of forgiveness.

The biggest lesson I've learned is that misery truly does love company and that I have the power to decide whether I'm going to live my life in misery or in peace. Maybe someday I'll write a book about it. You know what they say...truth is stranger than fiction.

WHO IS B. LAWSON THORNTON?

B. Lawson Thornton is a survivor. Like her character Kerri Mitchell, B. Lawson grew up in one of Washington, D.C.'s toughest neighborhoods. Drugs, crime and premature sex were the norm. In her early teen years, B. Lawson fell victim to the environmental hazards of ghetto life. By age 20, she was a mother to two children and married to an alcoholic, physical and emotional abuser.

Writing had always been therapeutic for B. Lawson, but after reading her own diary upon leaving her abusive husband, the author unmasked a hidden talent, creative writing.

At the age of 24, B. Lawson finished her first novel, *Misery Loves Company*. Though it was still in manuscript form, she printed copies for her friends and relatives, to which she received rave reviews. Convinced that the novel would serve as inspiration to women in unhealthy situations, B. Lawson started to research ways of becoming published. In 2003, B. Lawson formed East River Press, LLC.

Aside from writing and running her own publishing company, the divorced mother of two enjoys speaking on many subjects including teenage pregnancy, domestic violence and the effects of alcoholism.

SPEAKING ENGAGEMENTS

**Let B. Lawson Thornton
tell her inspirational story
to your group or audience.**

B. Lawson Thornton brings a unique quality to women that
have experienced physical and emotional abuse and women
that are or were involved with partners that suffer from
substance abuse. She also provides knowledge and wisdom to
those dealing with the effects of sexual promiscuity, and she
serves as an inspiration for young women that are trying to
overcome the struggles of having children at young ages.

To book B. Lawson Thornton for your event,
contact us at (301) 333-3956 or via postal or electronic mail:

East River Press, LLC
P.O. Box 4615
Largo, MD 20775

bspeaks@eastriverpress.net

BOOK SIGNINGS:

To schedule a book signing, please call (301) 333-3956 or
send an email to: blt@eastriverpress.net

FEEDBACK

Tell the world how you feel about Misery Loves Company,
please write a review on any of the following websites:

www.blawsonthornton.com

www.eastriverpress.net

www.amazon.com

www.bn.com

www.booksamillion.com

Express your comments, suggestions or praises to the author,
Send emails to: blt@eastriverpress.net

All comments are welcome

Available wherever books are sold, including:

Walden Books
Karibu Bookstores
Reprint Bookstores
Various African American Bookstores Nationwide
www.eastriverpress.net
www.blawsonthornton.com
www.amazon.com
www.mosaicbooks.com
www.bn.com
www.borders.com
www.booksamillion.com

Coming Soon from:

East River Press

BURNING BRIDGES, another intriguing and provocative drama from hit author B. Lawson Thornton.

CRAZY CAME THIS WAY, Tina Nickleberry's debut novel. This dramatic love story is guaranteed to hold readers captivated from page one!

For more information on these exciting new novels and to read excerpts, visit www.eastriverpress.net

QUICK ORDER FORM
(Send This Form)

Fax orders to (301) 333-5866

Payment Options for Faxed Orders (circle one):
Visa   MasterCard   Debit Card   Check Card

Mail orders to:
·   East River Press, LLC
B. Lawson Thornton
P.O. Box 4615
Largo, Maryland 20775
USA

Payment Options for Mail Orders (circle one):
Visa   MasterCard   Debit Card   Money Order
Certified or Cashier's Check

Card Number: _____

Name on card: _____

Expiration Date: _____

SORRY, NO CHECKS ACCEPTED

$15.00 + $3.95 for shipping

Make Money Orders Payable to:
East River Press, LLC